AT THE END THERE WAS YOU

a love story

WENDY HEISS

BLUE FAIRYTALE NOVELS

Copyright © 2023 by Wendy Heiss

All rights reserved.

Heiss Publishing.

ISBN:978-1-7391696-9-5

Cover artist: Katerina Zaitseva

Designed: Margherita Scialla

Editor: Jessica S. (Blue press edits)

Beta Reader: Lauren Dedroog

wendyheissauthor.com

To my brain. Thank you for keeping me up at night thinking of this story when I desperately needed to sleep and then causing me severe insomnia which therefore ruined my sleep schedule entirely. But, hey, we got this out of it.

Content Warnings

This silly little book came out of a little existential crisis I had, therefore, it might get a bit much at times, so please read the content warning list before proceeding!

Death, depression, religion, child neglect, scars, mention of self harm, mention of child death, mention of rape, ableism. This book also contains explicit content (sex on page), only suitable for 18+.

CONTENTS

Seven days until the end

THERE WAS VERY LITTLE Winter did not like about life. Waking up for the early prayer was one of them. And perhaps all of it. But ever since the night skies coloured red and the moon dimmed to a hue of grey instead of the shiny alabaster, she had found more and more to not like about the world they lived in. Sometimes she understood why the God of *Death* had threatened to end it, to kill every single part of it, to annihilate it, to send a dark plague that would wipe all of them off the land they'd grazed for aeons. What she didn't understand was why had he chosen to give them seven days until he'd do so. Seven days until the realm of Scelos would cease to exist. That is all that was left.

"Hurry or you will be late again," the High Priestess repeated the same rhymes and lines she'd said to her every dawn for the past four years, not at all affected by the news they had only learnt last night. That they only had seven days left to live, nothing else and nothing more, no details either. The Sanctum residents had very little contact with the rest of the world. "And fix your robes."

Winter pushed off from the only balcony on the Sanctum and descended the steep tower spiral stairs two at a time, following the long line of priestesses heading towards the prayer room buried underneath the ground where the God of Life had laid his first flower.

Late, she thought as she straightened her white skirts. Late for what? Would the God of Life deny them of it if they sent prayers a moment past sunrise? Would they all suddenly be left to be dealt by *Death*? Not a kind man from what she had heard. Unforgiving. Merciless. But so had been life most days, and Winter was not bothered by the cruelty of deities. She was not bothered by much, actually.

She fell in love with *time* at twenty, merely a year after joining the Uvralis Sanctum. Realised that it had soothed her into forgetting grief when her papa's heart had given away and when her mother's had withered slowly after from heartbreak. It had flown around her after own heartbreak. It had suddenly stopped when she'd read a poem or heard a song. Flashed with memories when she had longed. Changed to day when she had hated nights, and shortened nights when she'd missed day. Brought snow and then cherry blossoms again. Sun and then rain again. Once, she thought time had fallen in love with her back. As she was no longer afraid of it, counting it or mourning it. And she'd been enamoured with the marks it had left on her skin, each faint wrinkle and freckle was a kiss or a touch it had grazed on its passing. There was no tragic love though the end was death. She thought time had been enough for her, even if *Death* had not given her seven more days to live.

Miriam, the High Priestess, took the lead as always and knelt before the thick wisteria roots that had penetrated the grounds of prayer and even crawled all over the white stone walls surrounding them. The ancient plant emitted a melody, like the chime of bells at preparation school, it made her feel warm. She would often hum with it, and then be told off by the

High Priestess. Today, Winter was not feeling all that daring. Especially when most of the girls who had kneeled before it with their palms pressed together and their eyes tightly shut were sobbing along with their whispered prayers.

They prayed though there was very little magic left in their world. The deity who had grazed them had also left them soon after at the mercy of *Death*. Life was fleeting, perhaps that was what he'd wanted to teach them.

The prayer ended on the note it started. It ended in the same probability, too.

Unheard.

The girls all left and Winter waited until the last one exited the space before following after. A habit she'd settled for not wanting to look eager to leave.

"Winter," Miriam called her to a stop in the same stony voice she'd always used when she showed at the Sanctum after abandoning her studies and pledging her life to servitude of Gods. The old woman held her face passive, her chin high and her shoulders squared as Winter sheepishly approached to get the daily dose of reprimand. She was not quiet, she tried to be humble, she wasn't eager or went out of her way to pray, and all that made her a target for a lot of it.

"Yes?"

"Not *yes*, child. You've been here for how long now to know that sentences are spoken fully and loud enough for a thousand-year-old tree to hear."

"My pardon," she said, bowing her head and poorly mimicking her superior's stance. "I meant to ask, how could I be of assistance, High Priestess?"

The woman's mouth twisted, and she swivelled a look over Winter's body, clearly displeased with what she was looking at. Winter was an orphan like the rest of the girls there, but she'd once had parents, and Miriam had always hounded her for joining the Sanctum surrounded and filled by those who had only ever had the love of gods. "You have been called to the library. We have a guest remaining in our sanctuary. A Mage from the Charon Council. He has seven days to figure out how to stop...*Death*," she said bitterly.

Winter almost got excited at the mention of the library, the one place the priestesses had very little access to, unless it was to aid a scholar or a healer. Their prayer and holy books had a special room of their own, and according to the congregation, those had the only knowledge and entertainment the priestesses needed. "A Mage? And why me?" And why were those serving and praying to the God who'd promised to ruin them the solution? How can a servant of Death suddenly become its equal? But Winter did not ask that. She wasn't eager to spend the day down to the laundry rooms and scrub hundreds of sheets until her hands bled—like last time.

"He requested someone quiet. Someone who will blend with the shadows. You're good enough to be a shadow. And besides, I cannot afford to lose one of the other girls, we need all the prayers we can send."

Miriam knew Winter never prayed and had waited until this moment to let her know that she did. It should worry her, but Winter only felt relief, unburdened by the fact.

A Mage. She would aid a Mage.

Miriam spun to leave, and Winter finally let out a long sigh that she had to suck right back because other priestesses began flocking around her. Some curious, some agitated. But what bothered her was the few of them who looked at her with pity. No one in the Sanctum had ever given Winter pity. It almost made her choke up.

"I saw him," Clara, one of the young girls said. "He was tall and terrifying."

Winter would like to imagine that he was, however, she also knew that to Clara, everything was tall and terrifying. The trees, the Sanctum building, the handyman, her own shadow, all tall and terrifying. This is why she spent most of her nights either in Winter's bed or in her own bed with Winter in it.

The young girl clung to her sleeve and whispered, "I don't want you down there with him alone."

"He is here to help us and everyone in this realm, he can't be that terrifying," Alyssa, the eldest of their group said, trying to offer some comfort to their distress like she often did. Winter knew Alyssa felt a sense of responsibility to them, even to her. A very far night from then, she'd told Winter about her old life, the siblings that had been adopted while she'd been left...abandoned in the orphanage before Miriam had found her.

"Perhaps he will eat us all in our sleep," Clara added with a terrified gasp. "Our spleen can keep them powerful like that village woman said."

There were so many tales about Mages that Winter had lost count of how many versions of them she'd heard.

Winter giggled and everyone's attention turned to her. She tapped her stomach with a palm. "I'll chew on some rosemary. Make sure it's nice and tasty for him."

A few paled and one even fainted in Alyssa's arms, the latter gave Winter a hard glare which she deserved considering she knew half of the girls rarely saw the outside world and were terrified of it. "Shouldn't you be rushing down there by now?"

"Right," Winter said, and then dashed up the stairs towards the library building at the far edge of the Sanctum grounds.

It was an old building with three massive floors and an open ceiling made with glass from which she'd heard scholars used to study the stars. All three floors were open and shared that one ceiling.

The moment stale air and dimmed walls filled every sense in Winter's body, a rare smile stretched on her face. Stories, true or not, she loved them. There was no story of her own, not one memory she thought could be good enough to graze a page, let alone belong in a book. All the lives she had lived were those others had written for her to read. And it was good enough for her. It truly was.

She gently trailed a finger over the lines of dusty and mouldy books as she travelled the length of the shelved corridors to meet the Mage who had requested her aid. The notes of a distant piano filled her ears, and she closed her eyes briefly, enjoying the soft melody. Many feared the spook who had resided in the library and played the instrument for non-ending centuries, but not her. Often, she'd pass by the library only to hear him play.

"I presume you do know that is not how reading works. Staring, touching, and smiling at them is no help to me," a deep and cold voice spoke from her side, and Winter flinched, staggering a few steps away from the shelves only to crash on the one behind her. Surely, there would be a bruise where she'd hit her elbow against the hard oak shelf, it was all she could think about. That little pain was all she could think about even though her attention was solely on the man standing there and watching her as if she was the sole cause for the end of the world they lived in. Winter hated pain more than she hated *hate* itself.

Night. He reminded her of night. Black hair that fell a bit longer than how men normally wore it. Dark eyes, not brown, not anything black either, just dark—the look, the colour, the paleness of it all. Even the light stubble on his jaw reminded her of night. He was tall, at the least a foot over her, and she was not short by any means.

The dark haired man shut the book he held with a thud that reverberated all over the massive library hollow of any other living soul other than them. Who would want to read about living and not live themselves when there was so little time left to do so? He lowered his thin black specs and folded them in the breast pocket of his black jacket threaded with the most intricate designs she's ever seen. Nothing of his resembled any-thing of the life she'd chosen to live four years ago. Everyone in the Sanctum was blissful, modestly dressed, carrying a humble attitude that was no near a match to his cold one. "I presume you are Miss Winslow."

"Just Winter. That name does not belong to me anymore."

His face was so clean of any emotion that when he slightly raised a brow, it changed his whole face. It made him almost look...coy. Winter knew that the man before her could be none of that. Mages could never be coy. Only cruel. "Then follow me, *just* Winter."

"Will you stop *Death*?" she asked before she could help it as she followed after the man.

He halted his steps before they reached the only lit table at the centre of the library. Not even bothering to address her face to face like she was always taught to address someone, he said, "Do I look like a God?"

Yes, she wanted to say, *a terrifying one*, but instead she went with, "Does one need to be a God to stop *Death*? We stop sickness and disease, rain and snow and hail, we even stop happiness. How can we not stop something so simple?"

He turned then. For a second, Winter thought his eyes shone a different colour, one not drowned by the abyss of whatever haunting thing had buried its memories there. "Simple. Since when is death simple?"

"It is but the simplest. Effortless. Certainly, something we think of often, but we do not indulge it unless the nights are long or suddenly our skies feel grey or our heart feels empty. The thought of death is passing. Happiness is passing, too, but we chase it. Persistently. Constantly. We dream of it. Though we dream of death, too, but not because we want it." She chewed on her lip. "Unless it is one of the above again. It does that—death does that, it chases us instead, even if it is in our dreams. And when we wake up, we decide to not think of it. But if it was happiness we dreamed of, we recall it, share it with others, laugh at it or daydream it over and over until that dream remains like a sock with a hole that we often see at the bottom of our drawer but are reluctant to throw even though socks with holes can't be used much."

Now two lifted brows faced Winter, and she swallowed thickly. Had she angered him? Normally when she blabbered her mind off, people only sighed, ignored or yawned at her, they rarely ever got angry at her. She hopped from foot to foot and his eyes dropped there, at her feet. "Where do I come in all of this? The High Priestess said you've requested my help."

The man's dark eyes snapped to hers again. "Sit," he said simply and almost calmly, but his voice came like a sharp whip in Winter's ears, and she all but ran to take a seat.

A few dozen books were scattered over the round table, all open on random pages filled with languages, numbers, and illustrations she couldn't even begin to understand. How would she be his shadow if she needed his help to understand them? A haunting ghost, perhaps. Always tapping at his shoulders and draining him out of answers. Surely, she would be let go from this duty in a matter of a few seconds. Her parents had been well off and she'd received some of the best education, but it didn't mean she'd paid attention to it or been good at anything at that.

"I will not ask you to translate anything, don't brood," he said as he took a seat next to her, and she winced a little.

"What good am I for then?"

"Talking, it seems." He reached towards a book and placed it before her. "Highlight any sentence with the word *morta* in it wherever you see it."

Winter sealed her lips shut and glared at him. She wanted to know his name so she could curse him properly in her head.

"Azriel," he said, placing his specks back on and reaching for a few scriptures. "My name."

She let out a little gasp. Could he read minds?

"No," he gruffly added.

"W-what?"

"I do not read minds."

"How would you know if I was thinking that if you don't?"

"You're like an open book, Winter. Though I'd very much like to return to reading something else, so would you at least make an effort to not be one? Your mistress said you'd be a shadow, not the whole damn sun."

Heat rose to her face. "Apologies."

"I do not care for them."

"Then I take it back," she muttered under her breath, and Azriel's hand stopped in the middle of flipping a page.

From the corner of her eye, she watched his fingers adorned with silver rings remain still, her heart limping from beat to beat, worried she'd offended him. She did not care for the wounded pride of a Mage, but she was worried about her spleen.

She'd just lowered her pen to underline the word he'd requested, when he said, "So you can really read."

She almost choked on her own spit to rush out and ask, "Why did you think I could not?"

"Isn't it your sole duty to adore your God? The more ignorant one is, the more faithful they remain. You can question less when you know very little."

"Every girl in the Sanctum can read and write in at least two languages. And isn't it your duty to never question yours either? Not because you can't read, since all Mages need to first and foremost be educated, but because you aren't allowed to question the God of *Death*. My liberties have never walked such fine lines bordering to slavery, only adoration. You might hold a pen and a book just fine even if your eyes are closed and your mouth is shut. But can you use that pen and read that book out loud or at all?" She cleared her throat, and added, "S-sir." Instead of looking up and waiting for the coming reprimand, she dove to the pages and returned to her task.

"Can you also read *Kathran*?" came his question a while later, ignoring her rant entirely.

"Yes, it is my mother tongue."

He nodded and a book elevated in the air, dropping right before her. "Far from *Katra*, aren't you?" he asked, not paying any mind to her as he took dark notes in his thick notebook.

It was the furthest Winter could go without feeling the need to return. If she'd gone any further, the food would have been too different from the one she loved and the language would have been too hard to learn, so she stuck to where she was now. The language was not too hard or strange, and most foods were similar to the ones she was used to. She'd thought about it for days before locking her parent's home, not selling it as her old butler had suggested, and then taken the road to join the Sanctum. "Far is every place that is not home."

She had his attention then, dark eyes meeting hers across the table. Winter wanted to look away but couldn't. "Wise words."

Winter waved a hand in dismissal. "Read it somewhere."

"Thought you were only allowed to read holy scriptures?"

"Well, yes, but I only joined four years ago."

"Hm," came his vague reaction, and Winter frowned so hard her brows were about to snap her forehead bone. "If you're going to throw something at me, might I suggest a pen or a piece of paper," he said, paying very little attention to her.

"I was not going to hit you with anything."

"You looked violent."

"And you look like you've not had one good day in your life, but since we've met, not once have I thought you're about to cry on me."

"Are you always this argumentative?"

"Are you always this sour?"

"My answer is yes, then."

"So is mine."

"A pleasing outcome, it seems, since we both got our answers," he said boredly, returning to his study.

It had been about an hour of silence, or so it had felt, when Winter asked, "What are we looking for exactly?"

"Well, you are looking for the word death in The War History book. As you were when I first told you."

Winter wanted to curse him out loud. Would he turn her into a cockroach if she did? Did it matter? At least she could hide in here till the end of time. Which was in less than seven days now considering the clock had just struck three in the afternoon. "And you?"

"That is for me to know."

"I won't tell *Death* or anything. We've fallen out," her words dryly rang like the coo of an odd crow, or the squeak of cicadas.

He looked at her as if she'd grown a second head. Maybe she had, considering she was failing to control her own mouth from moving. "Was that a joke?"

She blinked once. "What are the probabilities that it wasn't?"

"Low."

Sweetly, she spoke to herself more than to him, "Aren't we in safe hands with such a distinguished Mage." He was still staring at her, so she felt compelled to add, "That was a joke."

More sounds of crows and cicadas rang between them.

"I gathered," he said drily.

"Will you turn me into a cockroach?"

He blinked a total of once. "Can they also read in this Sanctum?"

"I don't believe so."

"Then no, Winter, I will not turn you into a cockroach."

"I was joking, you know."

"I wasn't." He stared at her until she squirmed under the attention. "I presume you have another question."

"You presume right," she said, and then eagerly leaned forward. "Why did they send only you?"

"And you're presuming wrong in thinking *only* sending me is not sufficient."

Her nose scrunched from the sound of arrogance she was used to seeing in Mages.

He shut the book and lowered his glasses on the table. "Yes?"

"Oh, nothing," she hummed, tying back her long auburn hair, and returning to her underlining task. She could feel his attention on her, and like the most unusual itch, she couldn't shake it off. Surrendered, she dared a glance in his direction and found him exactly how he'd last been, staring a hole in her head.

"*Oh, nothing*," he boredly mimicked her. "What is that supposed to mean?"

She pursed her lips, thinking of how much trouble she'd get from already getting on his bad side merely hours after knowing him. "Ignore me. Most do."

"You're impossible to ignore," he said, and Winter's pulse grew faster. "You're standing about two feet away from me."

Her shoulders deflated a little. "I can stay further."

"And get on the bad side of some vengeful fiend hiding in this place? Much rather you remain where I can see you."

"They are peaceful."

"They might no longer be if they hear you," he muttered, going back to his work.

She looked over her shoulder, glancing further down the dark library alleys where fiends and ghosts usually found their gathering ground. Would they haunt her? She shivered, remembering how many times she'd run her mouth near them without care.

"Winter," he called, and she jumped in her seat, putting a hand over her racing heart.

"Y-yes?"

"Do you believe everything you are told by strangers?"

"You're not a stranger."

"You're not naive, but it seems you have a fault for not doubting intentions."

"Sounds like you very kindly called me naive."

"Kindness is not what I'm known for."

"Obviously," she muttered under her breath.

He narrowed his eyes on her. "Where did they find you?"

"I found them."

"That explains most of it."

Her lip twitched. "Most? Why not all?" she sardonically remarked.

But he answered, not regarding the mocking nature of her question, "You don't look like someone who'd believe there is a holier power that still cares."

"You're wrong." He wasn't, but was she that obvious?

"Highly doubt it."

"Sure, I don't believe any Gods watch over us anymore, try to interfere when things get bad or convince fates to change their course. I don't think they should do that either since we're given the force of will and power to choose over our own fate, whether bad or good. It is all life is about, the unpredictability. I'd hate to have someone choose for me, help me when I don't want to be helped, regardless if I need the help or not. But I do believe that the holier powers are not cruel. Why would they be?"

"And Death? Is he not cruel to decide your fate?"

"I don't wish to tell you my beliefs. You'd mock them."

"Are they so fragile in your beliefs that me mocking them would bother you?"

"No. But it might bother him."

He cocked that dark brow up again. "You think *Death* would be bothered?"

"He might be."

"And why would you care if he is bothered or not?"

"Someone has to," she said quietly, hoping he'd get the message that she didn't wish to talk about it. About the one sided relationship she had with the dark God. Often, she wondered why she felt the need to defend him when he clearly did not need defending, but she didn't question it despite never knowing the answer as to why.

"You can take a break," he said after a while.

"Will you?"

"I have no need for one."

She nodded to herself despite her wrists being on the brink of falling off. "Neither do I then."

"On the basis of my needs?"

"On the basis that this is clearly important enough for you to sacrifice rest. I will, too."

"I didn't ask for a martyr, Winter, take a break."

"Oh, but imagine when this is all over, they'd write books about me. The priestess who died of exhaustion whilst defending the fate of the world."

"Theatric."

"We have to romanticise our lives somehow."

"Why live in a dream when you can live in reality?"

Because it was easier, and in her mind, she was the one in control. "People never question me, you know?"

"But you say such questionable things, little martyr."

"Exactly. They fear if they get to the bottom of it, they will only find more things to question. Eventually, they all give up and let me be in my own questionable bubble. They don't question my interests or hobbies or curiosity." She fiddled with her pen. "Except you."

For the next few hours, she suppressed every thought and question she had, and returned to her duties of finding the odd word that supposedly carried the fate of the realm.

It had been less than five minutes since Winter had left the library, but Azriel had kept glancing towards the doors at least a dozen times. She'd not told him she was about to leave or where she was going, and he was wondering if she'd left because of something he'd said to her.

When he heard footsteps approaching, he immediately looked down at his work, trying to find the string of his study and failing.

A cup of tea was placed in front of him, and then a plate of biscuits. "Chamomile tea is good for headaches."

"What makes you think I have one?"

"You keep rubbing your temples."

He intended to leave it at that, but he simply couldn't. "Were you watching me?"

She blinked down at him, her face passive. "Yes. People watching is a hobby of mine."

"An odd hobby."

"It is purposeful as it is entertaining. People withhold telling you things about themselves, they shy away or plainly refuse to talk. If you look at someone long enough, you can learn to understand them." She pushed the cup close to him. "It will go cold."

"Is that important to you, Winter, to understand people around you?"

"Very."

He took a sip of the tea. "You put sugar in it."

"Honey," she said, taking a seat. "You look like you need

something sweet."

Azriel disliked anything sweet, but she'd not told him that she thought he liked something sweet, she'd told him he *needed* it. "From your observations, correct?"

She nodded and pointed to the biscuits. "Got reinforcements if that wasn't enough. Vanilla biscuits." Her eyes widened and then they shot up towards the open glass ceiling of the tower where rain was beginning to hit the surface. She smiled at it like she smiled at books, with longing. "Rain. We haven't had rain in months, I guess autumn is truly here. Not with us here, I mean," she mumbled, returning to her duty, and Azriel considered discharging her of it entirely, so she could continue looking at the rain with the wonder he did not think rain deserved.

He glanced up again, frowning when he couldn't figure out what was so special and deserving of such happiness. "You smiled at it."

Curious eyes bore into his. "I didn't smile at it."

"You did. You looked at the rain and smiled at it."

Her lashes fluttered fast. "I don't know. I didn't realise. Are you watching me?"

"The hobby isn't for me, after all," he said, reaching to pick up another book, realising that his headache had really lessened a little. He didn't know if it was really because of the chamomile or not.

Thunder struck the skies above and the whole library space filled with silver light, scaring the clingy fiends that hid between stories, away into their furthest hidden dark spots. The piano spook stopped playing as well, and silence filled their ears with an enhanced patter of rain that was heavily drumming on the glass roof.

"I would miss this the most," she quietly said, looking up at the rain again, not smiling this time. There was nothing resembling happiness on her face, only melancholy. "What would you miss from this world?"

"Not sure."

"So was I. But I'm trying to make a list."

Her oddness was seeing no end, and Azriel wanted to unravel that strange yarn of thought until the very end of it. "Why?"

"The girls were saying about a hundred things they'd miss if the world ended, but for some strange reason I couldn't find a single one. I'm sure I'd miss many things and many people, though at that moment I couldn't name a single thing. I am making a list now."

"What is on this list?" He forwent the *why*, too curious to know what she would miss to seek why it was so important to her to make a list at all.

"The sun for one, of course. The rain. Clara's screams when she sees mice and Alyssa's shudders when she thinks she's seen a spider." She giggled at the memory. "The feeling of getting inside fresh sheets after you have a bath. That scent of earth when it rains. Coloured glass. Bells, tiny bells that chime so dimly you'd think the sound was in your head and make you question your sanity. Mouldy books, they smell heavenly." She glanced towards the empty piano and the melody seeping from it. "I'll miss music. Especially your music," she said loudly to the empty spot on the piano stool where the invisible spook sat. Immediately, he began playing a cheery tune for her and she bowed her head in what Azriel guessed to be a 'thank you'. "I think that is about as far as I've gotten."

He cocked an amused brow at her. "Mouldy books?" Azriel had so many more questions. No one had made him question so many things all at once.

"No further comment on that one. We all like at least something we don't understand the reason why."

He didn't know if he wanted to dissect her mind, or soak on every little explanation she had. The realisation took him unexpectedly. He did not have time for anything unexpected.

The skies had gone dark with night and the library was entirely lit only by candlelight when Winter broke the silence and said, "I've done the last one."

The book she'd underlined floated between them at Azriel's command, and then one by one, the letters on its pages began lifting off into the air and floating around them. The words spun, hissed, and whispered around them, and Azriel's eyes followed them intently. Empty meanings, empty intentions and empty resolves surrounded the word death in many books written by the humankind. And it was all *Death's* fault for it. For letting them define it as they wished. For letting them think of it so lightly that they didn't fear sinning and hurting others and one another.

He sighed, almost disappointed when he emptied in his mind every sentence relating to the perception of death by humans.

"Is something wrong?" she asked almost in a whisper.

"Yes. I can't find a single thing that is right. All is wrong."

"I'm sure it is too soon to say so," she yawned. "You have six more days; you will find something. Whatever it is that you are looking for."

Azriel didn't know if she was positive or just nonchalant to the prospect of the world ending. He glanced at her tired eyes and then at his pocket watch, noting the late hour. He rose from his seat. "It will do for today."

She stood, too, stretching her fingers and wincing. "Will you need me tomorrow?"

His eyes were still on her hands when he said, "Thought Miriam had informed you will be accompanying me for the duration."

"She did," she said, masterfully hiding her hands behind her back and out of Azriel's line of sight.

"Then?"

"I thought you might want someone else."

Azriel didn't want anyone else. "You will do. Who knows what might show up at the door if I ask for someone else." A war horse? That was the only thing with more stubborn thoughts than her.

"I'm the worst they can do," she bashfully said. "Good night then, and I will see you tomorrow."

"Good night, Winter."

It had struck past midnight when Azriel stood from his seat, retreating for the day. His feet stopped before a cart holding discarded books, some torn and barely hanging on their spines and a few so old their pages had turned a dark shade of beige. He picked one up and brought it to his nose, inhaling its scent. Perplexed, Azriel stared at an empty wall for a few moments. "She was right, it is strangely pleasant."

Six days until the end

THE WHOLE DAY BEFORE, Azriel had spent watching Winter underline a word she did not know the meaning to. And she'd found the word precisely and without missing it in more than ten books the size of a brick. Her wrists had ached, and her fingers had cramped on more than just a few occasions, but she'd not stopped. He wondered if spite was such a strong feeling. Or was it anger? But from what little he knew of her, Azriel figured none were concepts Winter was familiar with. From the tip of her auburn hair that almost seemed brown under the library light, to the end of her white robe clad body, *just* Winter was anything but angry or spiteful. Strange, yes. The strangest human he'd ever met. And she reminded him of a flower he'd seen once long ago—too long ago that he'd forgotten the name of it.

But as far as he remembered, that flower was known as an early bloomer, it showed up at the first signs of spring, and Winter was late.

He'd almost felt her when she stepped inside the library. She brought too much light in a dim room. "You're late," was the first thing he said when she stepped over the threshold.

"Morning prayer just ended. I cannot come earlier."

He took her top to bottom again, noting the prayer robes she wore. "Ask Miriam to dismiss you of that."

"Miriam can dismiss me all she wants," Winter said, and then pointed a finger to the ceiling, forcing Azriel to look up. "But *he* won't."

Azriel presumed she meant the God of Life by *he*, but he couldn't grasp why she had just pointed at the ceiling.

"What duties do you have for me today?" she asked, stepping forward, and a flash of white around her wrists caught his eye.

She tried to hide her bandaged limbs behind her back, but Azriel took a glimpse and then frowned at himself, wondering why that bothered him. "Find the botany section and search for a flower."

"A flower?"

"It is small and white and has a yellow inside. Search for anything you can find on it."

She blinked once, twice, and then her lips parted like a rosebud. "You do not mean...daisies, do you?"

He stopped for a moment and searched his memory for the name. Had it been such a simple name? "Perhaps. I'd know that for certain if you completed your task rather than presented unsolicited opinions on the matter."

She pressed her lips together again and Azriel noted that was perhaps the only way Winter would stop herself from speaking, she had little to no control on her mind.

An hour or so later, the young priestess zig zagged through the library shelves like a bee, holding a few heavy books on her hands and a very bright look on her face that was enough to make Azriel sigh and drop his specs down and his head back on the chair rest. His temples thumped and massaging them did not help in any way, only added to that numb pressure his body was yet to be accustomed to even after living for so long. The cheery piano tune in the background was not helping either.

Slowly, he turned a hard glare on the piano spook, and the notes faltered, stopping all together.

Soft steps sounded close by and then something landed in front of him, forcing him to peel his eyes open and gaze up at the woman with oddest eyes—a strange mix of amber and light green. "Found it. I'm one hundred percent certain that the flower you were looking for is indeed a daisy." She blinked a little faster when he said nothing after a long while. "Have you changed your mind? Is it not needed to stop *Death* anymore?" Then her brows pulled together, and she chewed on her lip more viciously. Azriel felt the sudden urge to pull it from between her teeth and dig his own on it. "I don't understand why it was needed in the first place."

"Neither do I."

He could swear her eye twitched. "Aren't you on limited time to lose on such useless tasks?" There she went, Azriel thought, arguing with him again.

"Aren't we all?"

She swallowed again and Azriel felt another urge tugging on his restraint. He wanted his mouth there next. Instead of answering, she gave him a shrug. A single shrug which no matter how long and hard he thought about the next hour, he could not understand what it meant.

"You think fighting it is useless," he finally said, unable to bear the heavy insinuations, and she looked up at him from her book half covered from her hair pooling over it like scorching lava.

"Fighting to live is not useless."

"The thought of not fighting this does not bother you."

"Not really."

"Why?"

"Does it matter?"

"Why?" he pushed again, seeming to forget to soften his voice around her like he usually did. It frightened her, it made her wince and flinch, and he did not like that either.

"It is simply not my fight."

He didn't understand, and she didn't seem to understand his deep frown or unsated curiosity that she was not wanting to quench. "So, you'd surrender."

"We all surrender to death the day we are born. We just hope he is kind and forgetful."

"He is neither of those."

She shrugged again and Azriel did not like that gesture not one bit. "He is angry though."

"And how have you come to know that?"

"Why would such a tolerating deity be so cruel if not because he is angry? It is likely he is susceptible to emotion regardless of his title and power."

He ignored the later comment. "A tolerating deity?"

She nodded and he liked that one gesture better. "We fall sick and he allows us to find a cure. We become sad and he allows us to be happy again. He is kind despite his nature."

"Do you always speak such nonsense?"

"Occasionally." Her eyes rolled up again and stared directly into his, and Azriel liked that the most. He was feared and good at what he did, not many looked anywhere above his chin, let alone directly into his eyes. "You should, too. It is liberating."

"To speak your mind is foolish."

"To not speak it is a shame. With how little we live and how little we have to live, it would be the utmost pity."

He tilted his head to the side, regarding her, and her shoulders stiffened under his perusal. "Are you calling me pitiful, Winter?"

"Have you not at least once intentionally spoken your mind?"

"No."

"Then I pity you, Azriel."

Pity was not what anyone had ever felt for him. "You're a strange woman."

She smiled and Azriel faltered at the gesture, caught off guard by the casualty of it. "Maybe I do not pity you after all," she said quietly, returning to her duties. And then added, "How do you intend to figure out how to fight off the annihilation of all kind if you keep staring at me and not your precious books?"

"Is that what you think I am searching for?" His eyes roamed over her, over her pale bare neck and down to the lithe fingers that had stained with ink at the tips from touching word after word.

She gazed up at him, confused. "Are you not?"

"I know how to fight off death," he said, rising from his seat and pushing his specks back with a finger. "What I am looking for is a reason as to why I should do so." When her chest began rising faster and unsteady, he strode to her and watched as she followed each of his steps, not with fright but anticipation. Her neck craned to look up and him as he grasped the edges of the table and bent down a little to her. "Are you always this easily frightened?"

"I wasn't frightened. Wary, perhaps."

He liked how those words vibrated over his skin. "Wary," he repeated. "Why?"

"Because you are a Mage."

She didn't take issue with *Death*, but why with his human

servants? "Because I am a Mage," he again repeated, not understanding the young priestess with the oddest thoughts and who reminded him of a...*daisy*. "Do you take issue with all Mages, or just me?"

She'd bit her lip hard enough to make it bleed. "I wouldn't say all. Some, perhaps. A few. Surely, not all. I hope they are not all spineless crooks who do not care for anything other than gold, power and exalt."

"Surely," Azriel added, attempting not to smile. He sat back down next to her despite the work he had yet to complete. "And you've come to that conclusion, how? Met many Mages in your lifetime, Winter?"

"A fair share."

"A fair share of spineless crooks and all."

Her nose scrunched and she looked away. "Yes."

"A first love, perhaps? Someone who broke your heart?"

Winter's attention snapped back to Azriel; her eyes just slightly wider than usual. "Nothing of the sort. But they were part of why someone close to me died." Her eyes jumped here and there before landing on the books that Azriel had left forgotten on the other side of the table. "Aren't you going to continue to search for what you're looking for?"

He drummed his fingers on the table. Thinking whether it was worth even bothering with his quest any longer than he had. "How were they part of someone close to you dying?"

"Does it matter?"

Azriel crossed his arms and leaned back in his seat. "I shall conclude that myself, Winter."

"That someone I was close to was a Mage. A great one. Powerful as they come. Richer than rich. He was in love. The greatest love he could find. He was in love with power. So much so that he was willing to sacrifice his own life for it. Not caring who he left behind. Not that he knew what he was leaving behind because he didn't pay much attention anyway—craving, acknowledging and wanting power was all he was taught. Not only did he drown because of it, but he took someone else with him."

"Another someone who was close to you."

"Yes. Did it matter, then?"

"To you, it did, and it still does."

She sucked in a long breath and faced him again. "Do you think this will help us? Me telling *Death* a sob story. There are others with much sadder stories."

"Just because things can be worse than they are, does not mean they are not already bad enough. And no, I doubt *Death* would enjoy a sob story."

"Why not? You did. And he can't be so much worse than you." As if catching herself, she pressed her lips tightly together. "Don't turn me into a cockroach."

He leaned forward. "I've heard he's more of a gore indulging sort of man. Unless that sob story involves blood and guts, I doubt it would interest him."

He could see her chest rising with shallow breaths. "You're trying to frighten me."

"There would be little reason to frighten someone soon to be a cockroach."

Azriel had never felt such an urge to laugh as in that moment when her eyes rounded like saucers. He'd resisted the urge to laugh even long after that moment when he returned back to his seat, hiding a smile or two behind a piece of paper or a book.

After a glance at the clock behind him, Winter stood and left the library without a single word. She returned not long after with a tray filled with all sorts of pots and cutlery, lowering it on the middle of the table, sighing, dusting her hands on her robe and turning to him with a massive grin. "Dinner time."

His gaze jumped from the food to her, unsure of what she was asking of him. "Then eat."

"Eat with me. Or do you chew on paper like some odd seven feet tall mite?"

Azriel had never been pestered this much before, mocked either. He stared at the tray she put before him. Only stared at it.

Slowly, as if she was afraid she'd startle him, Winter grabbed his hand and put a spoon in it, even closing the fingers around the long silver handle. Azriel barely managed to focus on her words, too entranced by the way she was holding him and how she felt against his skin. "You do know how to use it, don't you?" When he didn't answer, she made a disgusted face and whispered almost frightened, "Please don't tell me your kind of Mages really eat spleens and stuff, and this is why you're looking at the bean stew as if it is offending you."

"What if I say yes?" he teased, but the tone was lost in there somewhere because Winter looked horrified.

She swallowed and stood on shaky legs, letting go of him. "Does it have to be human? I can see if the cook can find a sheep's or a cow's, at the worst a hen's."

"Why would you do that if it disgusts you so much?"

"You need sustenance."

He dipped the utensil in the stew and ate a couple of spoonfuls. "Careful, Winter. That gullibility is almost charming. No one would want to charm a man like me."

Slowly, she sat back, curiously watching him eat his stew. "I'm safe. You're safe from my charm, too."

He hummed. "Keep talking and perhaps not."

"Are you teasing me?"

"You think I'm a man capable of teasing?"

"I'd like to think so, or I wouldn't believe you to be human at all. And that would scare me more."

"You're lying to yourself."

"Oh, well, I'm deluded amongst many other things. So what?" she mumbled around a mouthful of bread. "They already think I'm a bit insane. You should see how the High Priestess looked at me when I asked her for shampoo instead of soap on my first day on the Sanctum. How would I know we were supposed to give up the luxury of perfumy liquid wash for the humble bar of mass-produced soap when we joined the congregation?" She squinted at the food and nodded to herself. "Though I think that crying when they burned my cashmere sweater had already labelled me as of unsound mind. I mean, burn my dress and my insanely rare leather shoes, but cashmere?" Winter sighed and pointed a finger at the ceiling. "Why is *he* against cashmere? Better yet, why does he want all our previous belongings burned at all? My cashmere sweater would have kept someone warm. Not me, of course, because *his* love," she said around a huge bite of bread, pointing to the ceiling again, "is supposed to keep us all warm, but definitely someone not fortunate to even know what warmth is."

Azriel was so confused. "Even food does not keep her quiet," he murmured to himself.

He saw a little light fade from her eyes. "You want me to be quiet?"

"No. I was only praising your resolve." He leaned back, watching her chew her food a little bit slower as if it tasted bitter. "You're a smart girl, Winter. I occasionally enjoy what you have to say though it deeply distresses me and sometimes heavily makes me question your state of mind."

Two red patches bloomed on her cheeks, and she hunched over her meal, shielding herself from him. "Eat your peas, they are good for you."

Azriel would rather ask for that spleen. "They are disgusting."

Her shoulders shook from laughter, and she coughed. "That is the most human thing I've heard you say. You almost gave me a fright there."

He didn't understand how that made him human, and he wanted to ask, but she clearly was enjoying her meal, so he decided to store that one question for later. Azriel was sure it would be an outrageous, an unheard conclusion, but he couldn't wait to hear it.

Once they had been done with their meal, Winter had brought him chamomile tea again. Instead of biscuits, she'd procured him a few pieces of dark chocolate. Migraines—she'd told him dark chocolate was good for migraines. This time, she'd stood beside him and watched him until he'd had them all.

It distracts me, she'd told him. *Watching others in pain.*

He'd not corrected her that he was not in pain because he liked that she cared enough to help him soothe it. No one had ever looked after Azriel. He'd usually been the one to look after others. After an hour or so, he'd concluded that he'd tell her that he was not in pain and make her stop giving him teas and biscuits and dark chocolates. He didn't wish to feel the need for care. What if the need never left him? Who would satiate it then?

But just when he was about to open his mouth to speak, she came to his side and put a cold compress to his brow. Stunned, he stood there, watching up at her with wide eyes as she wrapped it around his head and tied it securely.

"It helps," she plainly said, and returned to her seat. "I'll change it after half an hour when the ice has melted."

He was going to tell her. He swore it. Instead, he said, "I see." And then, not very patiently, he waited for that half an hour to pass so she could change it.

She brushed her fingers through his hair after taking off the compress, and Azriel's body went taunt at the soothing feel. "I'm sorry, it's all soaked. I'll get a towel."

He didn't stop her. Not when she returned and dried his hair when he was perfectly capable of doing so himself. "You've done this before."

"My mother used to get bad headaches. No one could even get a word in with her because she'd be annoyed at their sound of breathing. But the cold helped. I'd like to think so, at least." She bit her lip hard as if she was considering telling him something else or not. "Then I heard the maids say that she'd taken so much medicine, she'd be numb even after the grave." Winter pulled back, a lost helpless look etched in her features. "In truth, I'm not sure if it does anything at all. I just...don't like not doing anything."

"It helped." He lied. "Both the chamomile and this. I'm not so sure about the chocolate though."

Her amber eyes came a bit more alive. "I'll bring you more.

Maybe the dose was too small."

His stomach cramped at the thought, but he nodded and forced his mouth to move and say, "Maybe."

She folded the towel and held it against her stomach. "Anything yet? All you've read are history books, none that even mention events with *Death's* involvement. Should you not be looking at ancient spells or something?"

"Or something," he said, stretching back in his seat. "Any you recommend?"

She raised a brow at him. "A joke, I believe?"

"No, honestly curious you might actually have a spell *or something*. Do you?"

She scrunched her nose and Azriel withheld a smile at the smidge of frustration she showed. "No, but Francina, our cook, might. Her rosemary and onion soup can make you walk the lands of the dead and raise you from the grave at the same time. We can throw that at *Death* and just hope it works."

"That might actually be the best idea anyone has come up with so far."

"I'm going to pretend that was a joke."

He drummed his fingers on the table, and humorously said, "It was a joke, Winter. He'd most probably dodge it. The whole thing would be futile, and the soup would go to waste. Imagine all those people who wish to tour the land of the dead and be raised from the grave right after."

She blinked fast. "That was another joke."

Azriel raised both hands up. "Swear that it wasn't." He glanced at the clock and sighed. He'd kept her too late again. "Go. I will see you tomorrow, Winter." She had to leave, or she would never, just to keep Azriel questioning. He was starting to enjoy it.

Before she reached the library door, she spun to him again. "Do you not rest?"

"I'd hate for anyone to think I am a spinless crook who does not care. A few days without rest will not kill me." He knew he was no spineless crook, but he also knew he did not care, not even a little. And in five days, he'd be free from the burden he'd taken on his shoulders. The same burden he was still uncertain why he'd taken upon himself to complete when he knew finer men than him had rejected it, given up on saving what couldn't be saved. The realm was meant to die, and few had defied that fate. All those that had done so were only those terrified of dying, none who wished to live so much as they were afraid of dying.

Her mouth twitched and Azriel wished he'd said something else and prodded her smile to return, to see it just one more time for the day.

Just as she left, another shadow filled the periphery of his sight. The High Priestess remained silent at a wrongly estimated safe distance from him. There was no distance where one had ever been safe from him. But he usually allowed others of such a commodity, only for the peace of his mind though, dealing with fearful creatures was one of his greatest dislikes.

"Miriam," he acknowledged. "What do I owe the displeasure?"

"You left the library quarters last night. We agreed upon your arrival that you would not do such a thing if you wished to remain here."

So, she'd had him followed. Had she also seen whom he'd visited last night? Whom he'd watched sleep?

At the rise of his cruel smile, she staggered one slow step back. "I have no intention to harm anyone here." When he turned to face her, she staggered a few more steps back. "If you were so worried about the wellbeing of your acolytes, why did you allow Winter to be in my presence? Alone, at that. I could have had a town librarian brought here. Is she your spare?"

Her mouth opened and shut a few times, and an even cruller laughter left Azriel, the sound booming in the empty library tower that suddenly filled with shadows of dead souls and creeping monsters that normally hid in the shadows. "Seven days were too much. One would have been enough, you know. To convince *Death* that not one thing in this realm is worth saving." Azriel slumped in his seat and sighed. "How long will you disguise the rotting roots you pray to? Will you tell them that their adoration of Life will not make up for the decay of their soul?"

"Human nature comes with goodness and sinfulness. How can you blame us for our nature?"

"I blame all despite their nature if they will not take responsibility for their sin." He stood. "Pray harder, Miriam. Perhaps one of these days your *God* will listen and at least have a good laugh."

FIVE DAYS UNTIL THE END

SHE FOUND HIM UNUSUAL today. At first, she noticed his hair was not all dry after his morning bath that Clara had told just about everyone that she'd drawn it for him. Winter then noticed that he did not wear a jacket, only a black shirt that wrapped tightly to his hard muscled body, a few buttons undone near his neck that revealed a patch of black tattoos which most Mages wore—often as protection.

Forcing her feet forward, she reached his side and put the daisy she'd picked on the way there right on the page he was reading, breaking his concentration even though it terrified her to do so—to disturb him, not because she was afraid of him. Strangely, she was not.

Azriel lowered the pen he held and picked the flower up, staring at it as if he was staring at an ancient artefact. The flower was so small in his hand, it looked ridiculous.

In one breath, she said, "There are not as many of them as they were before when I was younger. The soil around the Sanctum is also mostly barren, and even if there were to sprout somewhat near, I'm sure the High Priestess would have ordered them plucked off. They are not that precious, you see."

"Why not?" came his gruff voice, and a small shiver travelled down her spine.

"They are too small, too plain, they sprout in between grass and sometimes even near weeds."

His thick dark brows bunched. "How does that make them ordinary?"

She sighed heavily, wanting to know the exact thing. How and why were so many things that brought small joy deemed ordinary. "Human perception is my guess."

"You are also human."

"Very astute. Though the High Priestess would like to argue on that. She thinks I am a ghost set to haunt her."

He looked at her then, his eyes raking slowly over her face. "She might not be wrong. I think you're haunting me, too."

Her fingers curled under the long sleeves of her robes. "I'd apologise, but you're not very keen on those."

Azriel went back to his books and pushed his glasses back. "Why would you apologise? Perhaps I like being haunted."

"You are a strange Mage, Azriel," she said faintly, reeling from his words and repeating the same thing he'd told her the day before. "And an even stranger person."

"To be deemed strange by you is strange itself."

"Let's agree that there is a magnitude of strangeness in this whole situation itself with everyone involved in it."

"But why?" he said, bringing the flower to his nose. "If we agree and seize to question all the strangeness involved, we might have nothing to say."

"Isn't that what you want so you can get back to perhaps the most important duty one can have? The lives of many lay in your hands."

"They do," he repeated in a trance, his eyes travelling into far away worlds like Winter's did when she sat in the balcony staring at the skies and imagined herself wanting something.

"It is quite the responsibility to put on just one pair of shoulders."

He set the daisy down. "Feeling sorry for me, Winter, or for the world?"

"Can't it be both?"

"Why not neither? What does feeling sorry really do for either of us?"

"Nothing. But it makes me feel human. To care is what makes us all human."

"Being human is what caused this."

"Did Death tell you that?"

"Death doesn't tell. Only show."

"Well, he should learn to communicate better then."

"Why should he learn to communicate when humanity can simply learn to be humane better?"

"You have a point."

He raised a single brow. "I do?"

"You seem surprised."

"Where have your sympathies gone?"

"I can still sympathise, Azriel, even if you have a point. You can still say you miss rain even if you love sunshine. I feel for those that have lost their way, I feel for those who have been hurt because of those who have lost their way. One way or another, at some point, you will either condemn the villain, become one, follow one, or live long enough to see them corrupt everyone else. It's the way of life. Unless you pick a weed out, whatever has sprouted around it will eventually die off."

He curiously tilted his head to the side, regarding her as if she held all the answers he was meant to find in his books. "Who will pick the weed out?"

"Someone who can actually see that what stands between

the meadow is indeed a weed. Weeds can look like flowers, you see. But the one who is able to recognise them, chose to pick the whole meadow even though he could see the weed, he's lost faith that the weed hasn't corrupted the roots of the other flowers."

"He might not be wrong."

"You don't truly believe that, or you wouldn't be here helping."

"Perhaps I was forced, coerced."

"You don't seem like one to be coerced."

"You're assuming."

"It isn't hard."

"How is that so, Winter?"

She pointed at him and then quickly lowered her hand at her side, clutching her robes.

He took off his glasses and lowered them on the table before leaning back in his seat and pouring every bit of his attention on her. "Is that supposed to mean something?"

Winter couldn't think of anything but the childish answer she gave him, "You're big and scary."

"Big and scary?" He tilted his head to the side, studying her. "Thought you weren't scared of me, only wary."

"Others are."

"They are smart. But that doesn't answer why I can't be coerced. Being something of fear makes people around you more courageous, fear is half as long lasting as spite and greed are. Humans want to prove themselves. How can they prove themselves with things they can conquer? Even *Death* can be coerced, even he can be forced with the right wrongful methods."

"Were you?"

"I don't like to think so, but I am not quite so sure anymore."

She chewed and chewed on her lips and on the inner walls of her mouth until the taste of blood almost made her gag. How come she had just realised the true severity of the situation? A messed-up thread of panic began tugging and trying to unravel in her chest, but the strands were too knotted and had no idea where the start or the end was. "Could it be that you are looking at this wrong?" she asked him, pointing at the pile of books he'd gone through. War history, war inventions, war memorabilia. History of weapons. Divine weapons. Human weapons. War and weapons. Weapons and war. All of it was making Winter feel unsettled. "Instead of wanting to fight *him,* why are we not trying to understand why is it that *he* is angry with us? Are we really to the point of no return with *him*?"

Azriel cocked his head back and looked at her under his thick lashes. "That is presuming that he is truly angry."

"*He* is."

His mouth twitched, and Winter braced herself for a smile, but it did not come. "If you're so certain, then I will task you to find it. From today till the seventh, that is your only duty."

She gaped, and then something she'd not felt in a while seeped through her veins, spreading despair all over her being. Like a flower under shade, she almost withered under his attention, and he noticed. The muscle in Azriel's jaw ticked when her eyes jumped all over the place, avoiding his, even though she often found comfort in their drowning abyss. "So, you were not certain in your guesses."

"It is not that." She pulled onto her robes, hugging herself and sinking into them as if they were her armour. The more she thought about it, the more she realised that they were her armour. The only thing between desolation and purpose was the stiff white cotton covering her skin. And the walls. And the certainty her position offered to never disappoint or do wrong. There was not much wrong to do in what she did, and there was no one to disappoint either. What Azriel was asking of her would strip her of that comfort, and she was not ready to disappoint or do wrong again. "What if I can't, if I fail?"

"What is the worst that can happen?" he asked, raising a brow, and flashing her the most unusual smile. "Die?"

Stunned, Winter could only stare. And stare. And stare some more. When confusion wrapped around Azriel and his smile was about to die off, she jumped to her feet. "Fine." Winter remembered that no single word was a sentence, and added, "I mean, alright, I will take that task."

"How agreeable."

She shrugged and Azriel's smile completely wiped off. "Don't shrug ever again."

Winter could swear her shoulders almost froze and fell off after his words. "Where do you think I could start?"

"It is your task. Why take the fun out of it?"

Fun? "You even know that word?" Winter muttered as she turned to search the vast corridors of the library. Her feet stopped when a dark chuckle filled the empty space. Carefully, as if she was about to scare a poor animal off, she turned her head and watched him.

"Winter," he called.

"Yes?"

"Why are you looking at me? Am I your task?"

Yes, she wanted to say. *I'd rather attempt every moment for the next four days to say or do something smart or funny and see if it can make you laugh again.* It seemed harder than fighting *Death*, after all. "No, of course not."

"Of course not," he repeated, nodding to himself. "Then again, you're not stopping, are you?"

Red hot embarrassment climbed to her neck, face, and ears, and she turned on her heels, almost running off towards the dark end of the library guarded only by dust, friendly spiders and odd fiends who'd clung to the stories more than the ink they were written with. When the letter 'D' came in sight, she slowed her step and began reading the tilted tiles one after the other, searching for the mention of him. As she pulled a few books in her arms, the question drummed louder and louder. For a moment, she could almost swear the darkness of the library echoed back. Why was *Death* angry at them? Why was *he* angry at all? Was she wrong to think *he* was angry? She didn't know much about *Death*, she didn't know much about the God of Life either, but the first had never interested her while she had sworn to serve the second when she wore her robes and abandoned whatever life she'd had before.

With a sigh, she pulled another book, forgetting the weight of the ones she already had in her hands, and dropping it to the ground. Afraid she'd damaged it, she carefully lowered the others to the ground and reached to pick the one that had dropped. Her hand stopped when she noticed the page that had fallen open. Though what she saw was nothing gnarly or ugly or terrifying, she shivered when her eyes fell on the dark drawing of *Death*. A bony creature veiled in black torn robes and with bright red gleaming eyes stared back at her. "Would he laugh if I said you're angry because you're ugly looking?"

she whispered to the drawing.

"Yes."

She screamed and then caught herself on the first loud note, slapping a hand on her mouth when she noticed Azriel leaning against a shelf, taller than any shadow on the library and just as terrifying. "Really?" she whispered, still breathing a bit hard from the scare.

Azriel cocked an eyebrow, seemingly confused.

"You said you'd laugh." She picked up all the books she'd gathered and stood. "You're not."

He tucked both hands in his pant pockets. "If you'd not screamed at me, I might've."

Embarrassed, she sprinted past him and towards the table, lowering the books and diving face first into them. She didn't need to force her concentration on her task like she thought she would have when he returned to his seat, something else entirely enveloped Winter as she read about *Death*. "They are brothers," she said, voice low, but he'd heard her.

"They are," Azriel answered disinterestedly.

Life and Death were brothers.

Life was weaved with golden threads and Death with ones made of shadows.

When both had bestowed gifts upon the realms, Life had offered all that he was, an endlessness of it. That was until it had been Death's turn to bestow his. Unlike his brother, he'd refrained himself from offering the endlessness of his own power. Could that be why? Because he went against his nature and did not take entirely, because he did not devour life wholly like he was meant to?

"Read something you do not like?" Azriel asked.

Winter's attention snapped to him, her cheeks heating when

she noticed him leaning back in his seat and watching her. Had he been looking at her for long? "Was he forced into not giving the realms like his brother was?"

"No. Whatever amount of his gift he bestowed was adequate to him. No matter how much of it he gave, everything would result in death. In the end, he always won."

That word surprised Winter. She did not know *Death*, knew very little of him, too, but would he consider that a win?

He cocked his head back, staring down at her. "You did not like that either."

"Whether I like it or not doesn't matter."

"It does," he simply said, pushing his glasses back with a finger. "But whoever told you what you want, think, crave, desire, like or dislike doesn't matter, certainly had you well convinced enough to make you believe it, too."

"But it truly doesn't."

"It does to you, Winter."

"I am no one."

"You clearly are someone. You're sat not even two feet away from me and I can most certainly see you."

"Of importance."

"You're important to *you*. One day you might be important to a friend, a lover, your child, a stranger, an animal."

"Important enough to mean anything."

"Again, you mean something to *you*. It should be enough. It is enough."

"Do you have an answer for everything?"

"No, not like you do. Only of the things I am certain of. There are few things I am uncertain of, Winter. The weather and human nature."

"Are you important to someone?"

"Certainly."

"More than one?"

"That would be a big party, would it not? I'm more of a lone cocktail sort of man."

"I think I am the same. Want to join me?"

"Who's paying?"

She laughed then. Like never before, Winter let herself enjoy the joke that really did not sound like a joke in his lips. "I'll pay, you greedy Mage."

He stared. At her. At her eyes. Her lips. Mostly there. "You're a priestess. I thought you do not possess anything of monetary value."

"I wasn't always a priestess. And I happen to be the child of a very rich family."

"Then why are you here? Don't tell me you found salvation in your belief?"

She winced. Many girls who were now her friends joined because of that reason. "Would that be a bad thing?"

"No, just not something I'd expect of you."

"Why did you ask then?" She fiddled with her fingers. "Presume, too."

"Because I was expecting you'd answer. If I presuppose something, you are more susceptible to answering because you feel inclined to debunk the fault I put in the suggested reason, and then give me a solid, but certainly positive piece of your mind."

She gaped at him. "Why do that?"

"Same as why everyone wants dessert after a meal. I'm craving something sweet. Thoughtful and with a unique perspective, too, if a piece of pastry can ever be that."

"Was that a compliment?"

"What if it was?"

"I'd pinch myself and then be flattered if I didn't wake up from a dream, possibly a nightmare."

"I'd say refrain from causing yourself potential bodily harm. If this were a dream, I'd not be in it, and if it was a nightmare, I'd be hunting you."

She nodded to herself, half engrossed in underlining her word of the day and half jittery from the words he'd just said. She wanted to question their meaning, question him, question the way he was starting to look at her and indulge her. "My limbs have not been made for running, I'm terrible at it. It would be a very short-lived nightmare."

When Winter took a careful glance at him, she caught him looking at her. "What?" Had she said something wrong again?

"I'd give you a head start."

"It is a nightmare, Azriel."

"A good one."

She narrowed her eyes on him. "You want to hear me scream and shiver from fear, isn't it?"

"I do," he said, standing and heading towards the upper floor. "Just not from fear."

Her lips parted as she traced his slow movements towards the end of the library shelves until he disappeared between them entirely. All of the sudden feeling too aware of herself, she glanced around as if searching for someone else who had heard what he'd said.

They had eaten dinner quietly. From time to time, she'd

thrown an odd glance at him, but then the piano spook had somehow caught her doing so and decided to play an ominous melody every time she had, so she'd stopped looking at him altogether. When Winter put the chamomile tea before him and then the plate of biscuits which she was sure he hated, he finally looked up at her.

Azriel took a sip, still looking at her over the simple rim of the cup and raised a brow.

"I could have poisoned it," she lightly said.

He took another sip, his lips curving into a taunting smile that had her squirm on the spot. "Have you?"

"I guess we will see."

His dark eyes gleamed and the smile stretched into a grin. "What else have you done to me, Winter?"

A strange sensation was pooling in her stomach at the way he asked her that. "Well, there was the poison, hoping you'd choke on the biscuits, the spiders in your bedding, and we can't forget the cold compresses. I'm trying to freeze you to death, though I think you might freeze us all to death with your icy stare instead. But you're smiling now, somehow."

"It must be the poison."

"It must." She chewed on her lip. "You didn't say anything during dinner."

"Were you waiting for me to say something?"

"I was wishing you'd sing me a happy jig, but I would be fine with just words."

He leaned back on his seat, one elbow propped back on the rest. "What sort of words do you wish to hear from me, Winter?"

She liked how he said her name, how often he said it. "Small talk about the weather, gossip amongst the newest Mage scandal that only a few know, and things of the sort."

"I'd rather talk about you."

Winter could feel her skin turn red. "What about me?"

"Yes, about you. Tell me."

She realised it then. "You were waiting for me to speak first, weren't you?"

He rubbed a hand over his clean-shaven jaw. "I'm not a good conversation starter."

"Just speaking is fine, Azriel. You don't need to be good at it."

"Fine for you to say, you're good at it. Starting and ending, both."

Winter was suddenly about to change her name to Summer from how warm her skin felt. "I just say what is on my mind. Dark and brooding, or not."

"There is usually nothing on my mind," he said, looking at her more intently. He looked like he had more to say, but he simply swallowed and looked away from her.

"Nonsense. Who can silence their mind?" She thought about it for a moment. "Wait, people can do that?" She didn't let him answer. "Why would anyone want that? To just...live with themselves like that. In emptiness and silence."

"It's comfortable."

"It's bizarre."

He smiled at her again and just held her gaze for a moment before sighing. "I might have to let you go for tonight, Winter. It's getting late."

Her head whipped towards the grandfather clock, her eyes wide when she realised it was nearly midnight. "It really is late."

"Good night, Winter."

"Good night to you, too, Azriel," she said, backing away

towards the exit a little slower than usual. She couldn't figure out why she was so reluctant to leave.

Four days until the end

She was late. Ten whole minutes late. Was she sick? They would have told him if she was sick. Miriam very reluctantly entered the library in his presence, but she would have told him regardless.

The door cracked open, and footsteps thudded towards his direction. Winter stopped a foot away from him, her auburn hair blown in the wind, and she only wore one sleeve of her white robe cover and was struggling to put on the other because her hand clutched a thick book that refused to squeeze through the arm hole.

Azriel stood and grabbed hold of the book and then guided her arm through the sleeve before buttoning it correctly. Her chest and shoulders rose fast. Too fast, he noticed. Did all humans normally breathe this fast? His hands slowed on the last button fastening near her neck and he allowed himself to graze the back of a finger over her skin. When she sucked in a sharp breath, his eyes lifted to her turbulent ones.

Her voice came out all breathy and low when she said, "Your hand is cold."

At her words, he did it again, he brushed his fingers against her skin. "You are too warm perhaps. Weren't you running?"

"I was, but you're also very cold."

"And you're very late."

"I know."

"It pleases me when one acknowledges their mistake." He stepped closer, unable to escape the opportunity to find out the scent of her skin too, not just the feel. His lungs filled with the scent of flowers. She smelled like a meadow and sunshine. "Are you trying to please me, Winter?"

Her throat moved against his fingers that were still resting against her skin. "I have a reason for my tardiness," she said, ignoring his question.

Azriel lifted between them the book he'd pried off her hands. "Does this hold the answers?"

She frowned at him. "Are you certain you're not reading my mind?"

"There is so much I want to know about that mind. Do you think I wouldn't have taken the chance and read it corner to corner instead of asking questions which you are starting to rarely or vaguely answer?"

Her cheeks stained red and Azriel fought to urge to lift his fingers there next. "There wouldn't be much to read. I don't have many answers to your questions, that is why I don't answer."

"Nonsense. You don't have answers that are perhaps deemed appropriate, adequate, pleasant, or agreeable, and you're trying to be mindful of your teachings here. But you have answers even to questions that don't exist."

"How do you know that after knowing me for merely three days?"

"How about you answer that?"

She frowned at him, and he liked that a lot. "Because you're a Mage?"

"Hm. You could've done better as a first attempt. Should I start pitying you? It is a shame you have such a mind to share, and you share so little." He didn't intend to mock her, but she might have thought so because she glanced away from him.

"How does this help in preventing doom?"

"It might, might not. Are you willing to not answer something that could be so detrimental?"

She huffed. "Don't pin this on me."

"Then answer."

"You know. You just know."

"I just know," he repeated, holding her hostage for one minute longer before stepping back and handing her the book. "What did you find out?"

With a shaky hand, she reached and took the book from Azriel, and then sat on the furthest spot from his. "The book spoke about folk tales detailing a few moments from *Death's* life which nothing else does. All books regard him as he is to be regarded—a God. They speak of him in exaltation and fear and humility, none go in detail of what sort of God he is, or even as a person. As humans, we've settled that dying is of course bad. But what of the dark God? What does he think of his gift? How would we know his anger when we know nothing of him at all. Nothing relating to him showing any emotion, whether anger, happiness, sadness. I asked a few of the other priestesses if they'd ever heard folk tales about *Death* because I had never. My mother never—" She stopped as if she had caught herself and looked up at him. Azriel did not give her the reassurance she needed, but she continued past her slip up, "No one ever told me tales, especially about *Death*. Everyone tells me they serve no purpose. Few of the girls said the cooks or the merchants coming in and out of the Sanctum might know a few since they are older, so I rushed to catch them when they were delivering to the kitchens this morning."

"And? Did they sate your curiosity?"

"A little. A few stories here and there. I was hoping you could sate it some more," she said carefully.

"Why would I do that?"

"You're a Mage and all Mages serve him, you ought to know some. Besides, we have one purpose in this."

"Do we?"

She hesitated, blinking a little taken aback at him. "Yes."

A smirk rose on his face at her perplexed expression. "If we had the same purpose, Winter, you would slit my throat before the days are up. But I'll indulge you."

Hopefulness filled her eyes until the black of her pupils ate around the amber of her irises. "You will?"

He nodded.

Excitement coloured Winter's face with patches of red that offered the most inconvenient distraction for Azriel because he really wanted to concentrate on what she was going to say. "What can you tell me first?"

"How about a tale told by a man who'd escaped him?"

She gathered herself tightly. "Will I be able to sleep tonight?"

"You can always join me, if you can't."

Winter gaped at him and then glared until he smiled again. "The tale you were about to tell?"

He stretched back in his seat. "At the gates of Asphodel, the realm of *Death*, roamed the three headed serpents. The past, the future, and the present. Each one of them asks a question to whoever crosses to the land of the dead. Once you answer them, they point you to the last fate a human soul meets—the afterlife. Hell, heaven or the lost in between."

"I thought that was *his* duty."

"His duty is to preserve the afterlife, not dictate it. He is merely a keeper."

"What happened to that man who escaped him?"

"A man showed at the gates, he had been a shepherd. Not young. Not old. Lived a boring life. Harmed no fly and wished no ill. When the three headed serpent asked him what he had been, what he was and what he would be, the man told them he did not know because he truly did not know. He'd only ever been what they'd asked him to be. Born the son of a shepherd and a housewife, being a shepherd was all he knew and all that had ever been told to him. Terrified of what that meant for him, afraid that fates would deem his life a waste and sentence him to hell, he fled back."

"How could one flee from Asphodel?"

"Death let him and warned him of a cost."

Winter's eyes widened. "Why did he let him in the first place?"

Azriel was lost in his thoughts for a moment. "I wouldn't know, Winter. Truly, I have not one clue. But he let the man return. Do you know what the man did when he returned to the land of the living?"

She picked on the skin of her fingers as she thought about it. "Searched for answers, chased after a dream or two. Found out who he was so he could have an answer for the serpent."

"Of a sort, but not exactly. The man went to the big city, chased excitement of all sorts, gave himself a shot at hobbies and meeting new people, even felt like he could fall in love again."

"Again? Who was he in love with?"

"He was already in love with the life he'd lived. After days of wandering worse than a haunted ghost, he returned to his village, to his dog and his elderly parents, and to being a shepherd. Without realising, he'd lived the richest life any man could ever live. Out in the wild, under blue skies and the radiant sun, with two parents who had raised him with love and adoration, who'd taught him to love back and be kind. He'd never been cold at night, he'd always had a shoulder to cry on, he'd never felt helpless or alone."

"Then what?"

"After giving goodbyes to his parents and animals, he returned to Asphodel, already with an answer to the three headed serpents."

"What was his answer?"

"He didn't know what he'd been, what he was and what he would be, because he'd been everything."

"Did he go to heaven?"

"He'd wandered back for far too long and his soul had detached from his physical body and remained back in the land of living. His soul probably still roams this realm even now."

"B-but why?"

"He'd been warned by Death that he'd lose something, and he did. There is a cost to every little action a man does."

"That is just...unfair."

He tilted his head to the side. "Did you change your mind? Do you still think him to be a tolerating God, kind despite his nature?"

He expected disappointment, but she looked frustrated, if anything. "What you told me never even made me doubt it for a second. Now I'm even more sure of it. I'm certain there was nothing he could do and that is why he couldn't let the man's soul back in Asphodel. It has to be. I mean, magic is tricky and all."

"He is a God. Maybe he could've just let him through. Broken rules he made himself. How hard can that be?"

"I make it a rule to not dip my biscuits in tea because I almost choked to death on the little bits when I was around eight, but I still break it. I cave and I dip my silly biscuits every so often. And every so often, I still choke on the bits. We make rules as a consequence of something. Sure, it can't be hard to break them. On the contrary, rules are so tempting and enticing to break. We break them all the time, or try to," she went on, barely stopping for a breath. "But there is a consequence. Like the man faced, he would, too. How do we know *Death* won't face consequences? A God like him would make rules to things with detrimental consequence, it is no dipping biscuits in tea with him."

He threw an elbow over the chair rest and lifted a hand to his face to hide his smile. "I don't know, Winter, that in itself is a pretty severe consequence."

"Besides," she said, her gaze dropping to the pages of the book she'd underlined. "How many times can he break his own rule before it is no longer the exception but the default? You said he makes no decisions, and that he is only a keeper. I'm sure he keeps himself in that position for a reason. It is easy to be partial in opinion. It is difficult to remain impartial. To be a bystander. How many times must he have wanted to say or do something but refrained from. I think I am right. He feels things like we do and cannot rely on what he feels just like we don't."

Azriel did not like that. Not pity, not sympathy, something far worse. "Don't humanise him."

"Why would that be such a bad thing?"

"Because there is nothing human about him."

"Anger is human."

"Assuming you are right."

"I assume correct," she said, pushing her nose up in the air, picking up her book and pen, and strutting towards the library corridor. "I'd like a moment alone. I'm not thinking many kind thoughts about you at the moment, and I don't wish to damage any Sanctum property when I throw them at you."

When she returned, Winter had changed her seat since they'd begun this morning. She'd started by shifting a seat closer to him when he'd indulged her curiosity with more tales of *Death* as a means to get her to start talking and looking at him again. A few moments later, she'd gone to fetch him a book he'd asked her to find as a distraction while he tried to calm and compose himself appropriately from the strangeness of all he was thinking. And when she'd returned, her seat was only a foot away from him. Azriel had noted her last move an hour ago, and his eyes had started shifting to her every two minutes or so, contemplating her next move towards him.

Her chair squeaked and groaned against the tiles as she pushed back and stood towards the corridors on the upper second floor, and he bit down a smile as he watched her pace back and forth, searching for her next conquest.

Unlike he'd predicted, Winter sat back on her previous seat when she returned, still standing a foot away from him. When she caught him glaring, she glared back.

His foot began tapping fast against the floor as he struggled to focus on the words before him. All but five minutes later, he stood and dropped on the seat right next to hers. He'd surprised himself more than her. For reasons still unbeknownst to him, he seeked her closeness.

She craned her neck in the direction of his book, her auburn hair spilling over his arm and grazing his hand. He couldn't help but feel the strands between his fingers, marvelling on the softness and the vibrance of colour against his skin. When he turned his head slightly to his left, his nose brushed against the crown of her head and his lungs filled with that soft scent of flowers again.

Whatever spell she'd cast on him broke when she asked, "Inventions of the humankind? That would help us against *Death*?" The way she said his name had always intrigued Azriel. His name came out as a whisper out of her lips, as if she didn't want him to hear her call out to him.

"No," he said sincerely. "It wouldn't. And considering what I've read so far, it would make it even worse."

"How?"

"I'm only halfway through it and yet not one single invention has been to aid the human kind, only destroy it. If you already want to kill each other, why is what he is doing any different?"

"So, you agree? He is angry at us." Her eyes widened. "He is only finishing what we started."

"You would be an impeccable storyteller." A pretty one at that.

"Why, you don't think that is it? You said it yourself—"

"I was only searching for something that humankind has not used against each other in hopes to find something we can use in less than four days."

"Something he wouldn't expect, you mean?" she asked him, almost...retracted. "To kill him."

He nodded and Winter's chest and shoulders rose faster. "Why kill him? I thought we only wanted to stop what he will do, not that."

"Death does not deserve your sympathy, Winter, nor does he need it."

"I wouldn't speak on his behalf. Perhaps he wants my sympathies. Especially when the highest order of the most powerful people who are supposed to be loyal to him have sent someone to find out a way to get rid of him entirely. What then?"

He didn't tell her that the high order who had sworn to him were planning things far worse for *Death*. He didn't tell her that it had never been about stopping the plague, but defeating him. He didn't tell her that they were about to use every little invention, humane or not, to end him. "Then you're free of him."

"No more death," she whispered.

"Exactly."

"And then?"

"What more could there be?"

She began breathing heavily. "Do we just live forever?"

"Would that be such a bad thing?"

"I...I can't. I mean, we simply can't. What would be the meaning of life?"

His brows rose. "Why would that be a burden upon *Death's* shoulders? Why is the meaning of life defined by him?"

"How is it not? It is in all senses. The span of it is decided by him. The reasons for living and fighting to live are defined by him. The need to live and outlive are defined by him. Life revolves around death, not the other way around."

Azriel realised it then, what he'd missed in her evaluation on the matter. She wasn't giving him sympathy. Not as much as she was asking of him to give her. "You don't want that, do you?" he said instead of what he really wanted to say, *You want to die.* He'd met people willing and wanting to die, but not those waiting to die. Some would argue that they were all waiting for *Death* and they'd find him eventually. But no, Winter had taken a stool and sat on his door and was waiting. He needed to know why.

Her lips parted and a sheen glazed her eyes, but she looked away before Azriel could make sense of it, of what it meant. "Doesn't matter what I want."

"It does. I told you that what you want should always matter, Winter."

"But it doesn't, does it?" she whispered, her lips trembling. "I am not the shepherd, Azriel. He found meaning in life, he'd always known its meaning. I don't think I ever can. But going to hell is not half as bad as remaining in this world and never being able to find that meaning no matter how desperately you seek it. To be left here with answers that you are nothing, were nothing and will be nothing for an eternity is worse than what we have to face after death." Her chair groaned loudly as she pushed it back and stood, fleeing the table towards the far end of the library.

He would go after her, but only after she had a moment alone. Azriel knew she needed that. He'd need it himself a few times before. He took that moment to think about what she'd said, about why she felt that she was nothing, about why she felt hopeless for her future even before *Death's* plague.

With a sigh, he closed his book. He already knew all he needed to know, all the ways the humankind could harm *Death.*

For a moment after he stood, he hesitated. What if he saw her cry? He couldn't see her cry—not her.

"I'm alright now, you can come," she spoke quietly, still buried beneath the darkness of the shelves.

He found her on the ground by the section with the letter 'A', holding a book tightly to her chest. Her cheeks were red, meaning she'd cried, and Azriel had lost the opportunity to bring her comfort.

She opened the book and turned it to show him the page. "I can't find your name on the name registry."

It looked like she still somehow had found comfort in him. Azriel crouched down to her, pinching a strand of red hair between his fingers. "I can find yours in about a million books. Why were you named after the coldest season?"

Her glassy tawny eyes dropped on her locks now wrapped around his finger. "I was born on the solstice. It was fitting. The midwife named me."

"The midwife?"

She nodded, watching him still playing with her hair. "My parents refused to name me. Refused to see me for a few days after, too, because I almost killed my mother during childbirth. They told the nurses and the midwives to name me as they wished."

He'd never felt anger sear his veins like at that moment. He grit his teeth and somehow managed to calmly tell her, "They did well."

"I think so, too. After I heard the maids in our house tell each other the story, I visited them behind my parents' back and thanked them. They remembered me. One of them had saved a few souvenirs over the years and one of them belonged to me. A handprint in ink. It was so small and adorable. I thought my mother would love it, I'd seen mothers gush over their babies and newborns. But when I gave it to her, she sobbed and tore it apart. It took her a while after for her to talk to me again. Father convinced her when we were about to leave for a ball held by Katra's mayor whom my father worked with. He said it would make us lose face with them if we behaved as if we couldn't bear to be next to each other. That night, my mother pretended she loved me." She fiddled with the corner of her robes. "On my eleventh birthday, I wished my mother would pretend more often."

A moment of silence fell between them. Winter did not say anything because she was still choked up, and Azriel was feeling the need to choke someone—someone who was smart enough to die before he came to learn of this.

"How is your headache?" she quietly asked, her small voice breaking the quiet.

He let go of her hair and stood. "Get up, Winter."

For a second, she just blinked at him and then quietly stood, placing the book back and righting her robes. "Now what?"

"You said chamomile helps with headaches. What tea helps with heart pains?"

She thought about it for a moment, and sniffled. "Jasmine?"

He nodded and turned to leave, only stopped by her hand clasping the edge of his jacket sleeve. One little move and he'd be holding her, touching her. "Where are you going?"

But she needed a remedy for her sadness more than he needed one for his anger. "To get some jasmine tea for you."

Her lashes fluttered fast. Her hand that was still grabbing onto his sleeve, tightened its hold on him. "No," she said, shaking her head and moving ahead of him. "I'll find some, you stay here."

Winter did not let him respond; she was already running away from him.

She needed more time alone, Azriel understood that, though he preferred she was somewhere within his reach. Perhaps it was better that she was not. Something worse than hatred had gripped Azriel around the throat.

He let out a deep frustrated groan when the piano spook began playing an overly dramatic rendition of something usually played during a horror theatre show. "Enough."

The piano groaned and notes briefly flew haphazardly in the air before stopping entirely.

Winter was hiding from him again. Only because it had suddenly struck her that she'd admitted one of her worst moments in life to a man she'd known for four days.

Clara waved a hand before her face. "Shouldn't you be going back? You've been in the kitchen for at least twenty minutes now."

Winter grabbed her chapped hand covered in cracks and calluses. "Why did Miriam send you to the kitchens again for the third day in a row?"

She lowered her head and started peeling the potatoes again. "I'm not good at anything else. She had us copy the holy sermons so we could give them out to the villagers, and I'd made about a dozen mistakes in each page." She shut her eyes tightly and sighed. "I don't know why I keep messing things up. It all seems fine in my head, the words seem fine, the letters seem fine."

Before she could help it, Winter mouthed a curse followed by Miriam's name. "You're messing up nothing, Clara. And we have typewriters, I don't understand why that woman is so against using anything from this era." She grabbed Clara's hands again and put them on her lap, tearing a rectangle from the side of her robe to wrap around her wrists that she'd massaged at least twice in the past five minutes. "Besides, to punish for mistakes goes against what she preaches."

"Didn't know you paid attention to what we learn."

"Can't help it. Her voice seeps in sometimes when I daydream."

Clara giggled. "Maybe you can get me some paper and a pen from the library so I could practise at night in my room. You could help me. I don't want to die not knowing how to write properly."

Winter's pertinaciousness on the matter did not dissolve, but she did soften at her little friend's glazy blue eyes. "Or we can just tell Miriam to go fu—"

"I agree."

Both of the girls spun towards the kitchen door where Azriel stood. Clara gulped so loudly that Winter winced at the sound. "I was just about to return."

His eyes fell to Clara's wrists still on her lap and then at Winter's torn robe. "Go to the infirmary and get a bandage and salve for your friend."

"Miriam does not allow us," Clara shot out, and then clamped her lips shut.

He almost...almost sneered. "She will today. Actually, you're dismissed from here, go visit the healer."

"We can't," Winter said. "Not unless it is utmost necessary for us to waste resources." How bitter that sentence tasted in her mouth.

Almost as if he'd tasted it, too, his jaw twitched. "I'll have a word with your High Priestess." He pushed from the door. "She won't have much use for those resources if all perishes in three more days."

Winter gave Clara a nod and then followed after him towards the library. "I didn't mean to stay so long."

"It is good that you came to your friend."

"Good for what?"

"Comfort."

"I-I didn't come to get comfort."

"Your way of getting comfort is by giving it. Odd, but there isn't anything ordinary about you, Winter."

She stopped walking, dazed by the fact that he knew her better than what she chose to know herself, or acknowledge. "I'm very ordinary."

He stopped a few feet away ahead and slightly turned to her. "If you insist."

When she made to step past him, he blocked the door entirely, her chest bumping on his.

He caught her before she fell, his hand planted firmly on her waist. "You're done for today."

She couldn't form a single thought. Not when he was touching her. "It is only five in the afternoon."

Very slowly, he pulled his hand away from her, his fingers lingering a little over her body. "Spend it with your friend. Spend it in the rain, smiling or sulking at it, whichever you want. You look pretty while sulking, too."

Winter's lips parted as if to say something, but she only sucked in a sharp breath and closed them as she stared at him. "And you?"

"I'll finish early, too. If I am lucky, I might get to see you sulk or smile at the rain."

It had not rained. There had been no sun either to smile or sulk at it. But Winter wanted to do neither and watch neither. Not when Azriel was watching her from the massive library window as she and her friends laid on the ground. She wanted to smile and sulk at him instead. She would have looked in his direction and done both, but Miriam was watching her and her friends like a hawk as they bathed in the chilly autumnal air, laying on a pile of fallen leaves and staring above at the clouds, trying to make out the most outrageous shapes out of them.

Clara had found some bird and animal shapes. Alyssa had made out an object or two, but all Winter could see in the clouds was...clouds. It was odd. Winter could almost always force her mind to make something up, to imagine. Not today. She tried and tried even after her friends had gone inside, even after the skies were no longer visible under the dark night.

She'd just closed her eyes when she felt a shadow falling over her. When she opened them, a pair of black eyes were looking down at her. Night was looking down at her. The darkest night. Starless. Moonless. But the most entrancing one she'd ever seen.

Without helping it, she smiled up at him while he frowned even deeper and looked up at the skies as if searching for the reason of her sudden joy there.

"You finished early," she said.

He looked back down at her. Night did. "Your eyes were

closed."

"There is no sun or rain, I had to imagine it, but I wasn't doing a very good job."

"Then why are you smiling?"

"Not exactly sure."

"Tell me when you figure it out."

"Alright." Before he turned to leave, she asked, "Why did you come out?"

"I thought you'd fallen asleep."

She smiled again. "Were you going to come and smother me?"

"Why would I do that to the poor woman who I'm turning into a cockroach?"

Winter was now grinning at him and that somehow always made him frown like he couldn't make sense of it. "Take care of me when you turn me into a cockroach, will you?"

He finally lowered himself down to her, crouching just above her, their faces closer. She thought him handsome even upside down like that. "Presuming I'd keep you."

"You'd keep me."

He reached a hand to her face and carefully pushed a strand of hair away from her eyes. "Go to bed, Winter. It is getting late."

"I will, only because you're much nicer in my dreams."

His lips twitched with amusement. "Am I?"

"No. I lied. You're the same there, too."

He smiled then. Alas, it was very faint and dark and just as brooding as the rest of him, but he was smiling—at her. "I'm nothing if not consistent."

"Thank you for today."

Azriel's demeanour shifted entirely, and if it had been still day and bright, Winter would have mistaken him for the darkest thundercloud. "Nothing to thank me for, Winter."

She pushed up and stood, turning to him after dusting off all the dry leaves from her robes. "I decide that."

"Have a good night, Winter," he said, standing to leave.

"No. I've decided against it."

He stopped and looked over his shoulder at her. "Decided against having a good night?"

"Yes. I want to have a bad one. Live in your shoes for once and see how the other miserable unthankable side feels."

His head lowered and his shoulder started shaking. Still somewhat baffled, Winter realised it a tiny bit too late that he was laughing. Azriel took off his glasses and rubbed hand over his eyes, grinning. "Alright, Winter, no need to go that far, I'll apologise."

"For what?"

"For deciding what you can or cannot be thankful for."

"Thought you didn't care for apologies."

"But you do." He put his glasses back on and turned away from her. "Go to bed now."

She had gone to bed right after he'd told her to, but she'd not been able to fall asleep for long after. Thinking. Thinking of the past four days. She couldn't find anything to think of prior to them. So, she'd stayed up late to come up with a reason why nothing had been memorable enough for her to remember before these four days, and why these four days had so much for her to think about.

THREE DAYS UNTIL THE END

HE LOOKED TIRED WHEN she returned to the library on the fifth day. Something rested heavily on Winter's chest when she looked at him in this new dishevelled form that she was sure no one had ever seen him in. There was much certainty in her thoughts concerning him. Like he'd asked the other day, she also just knew about him—it was like a sense, a foreboding that scared her senseless.

Not bearing it any longer, she reached him and took his hand before she had time to think against it. "Let's spend an hour outside. I miss the sun and it's finally out today."

"Have a break and go stay in the sun for a little while. Take your friends, too," he said, but still held onto her hand, his thumb working back and forth over her skin, so softly and tenderly that gooseflesh chased up her arm and then all over her body.

Winter shook her head and pulled onto his hand until he had no choice but to get to his feet. They were so close that her neck ached at the angle when she looked up at him. "Take your book. Contrary to popular belief among corpses like yourself, you can also read outside."

He leaned down until his face was entirely too close to hers that she could taste his scent of vetiver and sandalwood on her tongue. "Is it so?"

She nodded and made to pull away from him before her mouth would start watering just for a little taste of his skin, but he held onto her tightly. "You're holding my hand."

"I suppose that is what they call it when two people join their hands."

"Why are we?"

"Any objections?"

Still dazed, she answered, "None."

"Winter," he called to her, and she snapped back to attention. "You were about to take us somewhere."

"Right." She closed her fingers around his hand and pulled him out of the library and towards her room to fetch a blanket.

Azriel stood like an anomaly in the middle of her room, observing the hollow space made of four walls, one small window, a bed and a small table. It had surprised her the same when she'd seen it for the first time. How much she had left behind in her old life made of rosy walls and fresh flowers on every nook her mother could fit. She'd been sheltered within those same rosy walls which had been covered in tar from the outside.

"They lock you in here?" he asked her.

Her laugh was half uneasy and half embarrassed. "No, they do not lock me."

"Looks like a prison cell."

"I'm sure even prisoners are grateful to have a warm bed."

"Yes, but you aren't a prisoner, are you?"

At times, she thought. "I do not ask for more. It satisfies me."

"Satisfies," he hummed her words as he studied the small objects on the odd table where she had her meals or sat to read and write. Picking up the book resting there, he turned to face her. "You said tales are useless."

"It is said that they are useless, I do not think it."

"Did you find this in the library?"

"No. It belonged—" She stopped herself at that. "It was...uhm, my mother bought it." Only bought it, she'd never read it to Winter. In fact, she wasn't entirely sure if her mother had even bought it for her on her seventh birthday. Her mother had seemed surprised at the book when she'd unwrapped it, and then had sent a scathing and disapproving look towards the maids. But she liked to think and pretend her mother had chosen it for her.

"So it was your mother's."

Her lips quivered when she forced them to whisper the word, "Yes."

He cracked the book open and began flipping through the pages of the only possession from her old life that she'd kept. "The mention of her saddens you."

She fiddled with the side of her robe, picking at the threads. "I'm not certain if it does."

Azriel looked up from the page and pinned a strange look on her. "Grief is a given when you lose someone you care for, is it not?"

"I did not lose my mother. You cannot lose someone who did not want to be here. Especially someone who did not care to stay behind for me." Winter was not sure if her mother had even considered her at all when she'd taken her own life right next to her room, just one wall away. She'd not considered that her daughter would find her first, and that she'd be the one to not feel her pulse or hear her breathe. Her mother had never considered that Winter's white slippers would never be white again after they'd soaked in her blood, or that Winter would never forget the exact colour of blood or the exact way her mother's eyes had sunk to a bottomless pit of grief.

"So, the memory of her angers you."

She shook her head, and Azriel narrowed his eyes on her. "No, I'm not angry at her either." Winter couldn't be. Not after—no, she couldn't be at all because she'd also been selfish before and she understood how needy that feeling was.

"Then what are you, Winter?"

"Neither sad nor angry. That is all I know."

"Could it be because you know how to be neither of those?"

Her fingers froze at her side, letting go of the thread she'd pulled. "I know how to be angry."

"Not at yourself, at others."

"That, too."

"Why are you never angry at me?"

"Why would I be angry at you?"

"Many are." He reached to push a strand of wild hair behind her ear. "So you've been sad before."

She shrugged and then bit her lip, forgetting he'd told her not to.

"The Mage was your father," he said matter of factly.

"He was."

"And your mother died after he did."

She took a deep breath. "She did."

"And you?"

Her eyes found his, as if looking for her answers there. "What about me?"

"Where were you left in this negative equation?"

"Here," she replied meekly.

"Here," he repeated like he always did. She often wondered if it was because he truly couldn't grasp the meaning of the word. "Where is it that you want to be?"

"I don't know. No one ever told me anything. For as long as I lived, I followed their orders. Ate when they asked me to eat, slept when they asked me to sleep, only cried when they'd let me cry, laughed only when it was appropriate to laugh. Then they left and I didn't know who to ask and no one would tell me anything."

"Is this why you joined the congregation?"

She pointed to the ceiling and asked in a hushed voice, "Would *he* turn me into a cockroach if I said it out loud?"

Azriel shrugged. He *shrugged*.

"Yes," she whispered. "After they passed, the first time I felt relief was when I came here. It is ridiculous, I know."

"Wanting to find purpose is not ridiculous, Winter. What's ridiculous is the fact that you were ripped of the choice."

"My parents were of high status, mingled with the rich and the powerful, sat high in the ladder of faculty, so anything I did wrong, they did wrong. They didn't rip me of the choice. I chose to obey them." *Because she didn't want to disappoint or fail them*, Winter omitted from her answer.

"Choose and force do not share a meaning."

"They did not force me."

"No, maybe not, but taking away your ability to even have other choices isn't exactly so far off."

Winter's lips parted, ready to answer, but the answer did not come. He was right. "And you?"

"What about me?"

"Did you have choices?"

His smirk was almost wicked. "Many."

"Coming here to look for a way to fight off *Death*, was that a choice you made?"

"Yes."

"You didn't look too pleased and it is not that you are trying hard enough to match the severity of what is asked of you."

"Some choices, Winter, they get better or worse when you make them. You can regret making choices. You can make mistakes in choosing. You are allowed. But to do all that, you have to have choices."

"So you regret coming here?"

There was a pause as he stared at her, and said, "Not even a little." He put the book on the table and leaned against it, sliding his hands in his pockets. "What were they like? Your parents." From the way he grit his teeth at the word *parents*, Winter knew he wanted to add more to that question.

He'd not asked her anything difficult, but she couldn't find the words for an answer. Of course she knew them. She knew what they liked and how they smelled and who their friends were and their favourite foods, she even knew her mother's favourite colour. She knew so many things that it could take her days and weeks to list. So why did she say, "There."

"There?"

"They were just...there."

"Did they love you in the end?"

The question took her aback. Then she remembered the words she'd told him the day before. "Of course they did," she said with an incredulous smile, but felt her eyes burn. "All parents love their children."

There was no emotion on his face when he said, "Not mine."

Her feigned smile fell entirely. "Why not?"

"I do not care for their reasons." He swivelled another slow look over the room, almost lost in thought. "And you, did you love them?"

"Yes, I did." With all she had, and so much more. "You?"

He paused at her question and looked at her. His eyes were so cold, so dark, with so many shadows. "In the end, it doesn't matter if we love them or not if they do not love you back."

Winter was astounded for a moment. The answer was so unlike him even though it seemed like an answer he'd give. "That is not true."

He pushed from the table and closed the small space between them entirely. "Why is it not, Winter?"

"Because you said it matters what we want, like, think, desire, love."

He smiled at her. He really smiled at her and brushed his fingers over her cheek. "Very well. You learn well."

Winter had been touched, but never that gently, never from such cold gentle hands. "Will you not answer me truly? Did you not love your parents?"

"It would change the way you look at me."

"How so?"

"Because I didn't."

She nodded to herself. "You must have a reason."

"Not everything has a reason."

"Tell me this does."

"It might not be enough."

"Azriel."

His hand stopped on her cheek, his thumb slightly grazing her bottom lip, and she briefly lost the ability to breathe. "They made me become something of fear. Something that only brings chaos and pain when I was incapable of inflicting either of them."

"I see." She truly did. Winter did not know the Azriel outside the Sanctum grounds; she didn't need to, though, to know that he was none of the things he thought his parents had made him.

"You believe me?"

"Why shouldn't I?"

He stepped closer to her. Closer than he'd ever been to her. He rested his forehead on hers, and breathed out, "So many reasons, Winter. So many reasons."

"Exactly. Reasons. You have them," she whispered back. She didn't want to share that moment and those words with anyone but him, not even the wind.

He stepped back first, and Winter refused to look at him after that moment. She didn't know if she could without never wanting to look away.

After retrieving a blanket from her wardrobe, she pulled onto Azriel's hand and tugged until both were heading towards the back gardens where no one usually perused, afraid of the forest that was too close to it. Winter had never been afraid of it. Not because she thought herself above bears and wolves, but because she'd read over a dozen books specifying that the forest housed no such fauna. Convincing the others was no concern of hers, and besides, she liked the company of no more than one. Just not today. Today she liked the thought of bringing Azriel to her sanctuary.

The man in question glanced around the area as if it was above the ordinary, his eyes jumping to some of the most random details. An odd dandelion half blown by the wind, a distant coo of an owl, the dried maple leaves that had not been cleared by the gardener yet because Miriam wanted all the trees to shed before calling on their services. But what seemed to impress him more was the fact that she laid the blanket on the grassy floor and sat down on it. Impressed was not the right word for it, he looked baffled, stunned at the prospect of sitting on the ground.

Winter patted the space next to her, and he immediately sat down as if he'd not judged her for it not even a second ago.

"Are all Mages allergic to the sun?"

Azriel squinted when he turned to give her a look. "They should be. It is hideous." His hand shot forward and tangled in her hair, and she froze still as he studied her locks, ignoring the trail of goosebumps that chased down her neck the caress caused. "It changes colour in the sun." But he was not done like Winter thought. His other hand moved to cup her face and titled it up to him. His skin was icy against hers. "And you have freckles. More than I thought." He stopped for a moment, gazing straight into her eyes as if he was seeing them for the first time. "You're a stunning creature, Winter."

Her face heated at the words and his touch and his attention that she held like a compass pointing north. "You're cold."

Azriel let go of her face and hair, and stared at his palms for a moment. "And you're too warm. Are all human beings this warm?"

Winter couldn't help it. She laughed. And he stared this time—at her, at her eyes, her mouth, mostly there. Clearing her throat, she gathered her knees to her chest and returned her attention to the book she'd picked. "You can read now, I won't disturb."

"What if I want to disturb you?"

Her pulse went on a run again. "I cannot allow you to do that. The lives of many rely on you solving this."

"I'll save them all if you pay attention to me."

She turned and offered him a coy smile. "Oh, so now the realm's fate lies at my fingertips?"

"Not exactly." He took her hand and put it to his cheek. "Now it does."

"You're cold." She didn't know why she kept repeating that phrase, not that it mattered at all because she liked his touch, she liked the chill it sent over her, she liked that she burned less.

"So you keep saying." He nuzzled her palm and pressed a kiss at the edge before he let go of her. "Will you let me disturb you then?"

Winter's heart leaped along with her breath, still feeling his lips on her skin, and that burn grew intense again. "I do as you say."

His eyes gleamed. "Come here then."

"Where?"

"Close to me."

"Why?"

His mouth titled into a smirk. "Because you do as I say."

She got on her knees and crawled close to his side, something that he liked because he followed her movement closely and with too much relish.

Azriel took his jacket off and her eyes glued on him when he rolled his sleeves to reveal lines and lines of dark tattoos marking his skin.

"What do they mean?" she asked. "The markings. I can't recognise the language."

"It is the oldest one there is."

"*Maloori*?" No longer spoken, only used by a few very powerful Mages to cast their magic with. Said to have been brought from Asphodel.

"Older."

Winter frowned. She didn't know there was a language that old.

He took her hand and guided her finger across the odd letters. "I am only what I can be. What it reads."

She licked her dry lips. "And what is that?"

"How about I let you figure that out? On the seventh day, tell me what I am."

Something was wrong with Winter—very wrong. "Don't I have to know you to answer that?"

"You can know me."

"Do you truly believe we are not worth saving, is that why you are not trying harder to work out a solution?"

"Yes."

She gathered herself tightly. "Maybe they should've sent someone else."

"There was no one else to send to find something that does not exist."

"What does that mean?"

He leaned back until he was laying down on the blanket, both hands under his head as he stared up at the strange skies that were beginning to murk over. For a moment, his eyes turned grey from their reflection. "What they call *humanity*."

"It is not something you can search in books, let alone find it there."

A strange look passed over his stark face when he looked at her. "Indeed."

"Then why did you seek it there in the first place?"

"It was something I had only read and heard about. Never seen. I had little hope to find it elsewhere. Aren't you going to ask why it is that I am looking for?"

"It would never make sense to me as it does to you. You're a Mage, and I am not." She chewed on her lip and then stopped when she noticed Azriel's attention dropping there. "You said you've never seen it? How have you never seen humanity?"

"Have you?"

Winter hesitated for a moment. She debated how sure she was of her answer before she went with a meek, "Yes."

"From who?"

"From many. Take Alyssa, for one, she is one of the priestesses here. She always made sure I had enough to eat and drink, and that I wasn't cold at night even when she knew nothing of me. She always comforted me, pulled me aside when she felt something was wrong, stayed with me at night when I couldn't sleep."

"Because that is her duty as a servant of her God."

"Not necessarily. Not all was her duty." She laid on her side facing him, their faces only inches apart. "Think about it, Azriel. The action itself is humane, is it not? The fact that it becomes a duty to obtain reinforces it. To know right and wrong, good and bad, knowing to act on that same basis of knowledge is what humanity is all about. People sometimes are tired, heartbroken, starved, sick, deliriously happy or over-joyed, other states of mind where inhibition is stolen from you, they might act upon how they feel at those moments, but acting upon those feelings is the most human thing one can do. Not all is inherently bad."

"Not all is good either."

"But we shouldn't assume some can't be."

He trailed the back of his hand down her jaw. "If Death saw the world with that amber colour lens of your eyes, little sun, he'd be doomed. He'd start sending people back to the land of the living before they stepped on the gates of his land."

She was trying very hard not to smile. No one had ever given her a nickname before. Winter reached to touch him as he was touching her. "He has a duty to hold. He is part of nature, born as it. No one blames him for what he does or what he is. Asking him to look at us another way would do us more harm than good, he only has to keep looking at us as he has."

"I think these eyes would change his mind."

"My world is sometimes grey, he wouldn't like it."

He turned to her fully, his hand spanning across the nape of her neck. "Who would dare paint it as such?"

"Me. I can have all the colours lined before me, and I'd still dip my brush in grey. If you ask me why, I wouldn't be able to answer you. If you ask me if I hated colour, I would say not always. If you asked me to try and dip my brush in them, I'd tell you that I hate it and then I'd resent you for forcing me to do so. Everyday, I see the world differently. Sometimes I hate it, resent it, love it, adore it. If I decided the fate of the world on the basis of what day it is, the world would have ended long ago. I'm sure Death is susceptible to grey days, too. He's existed a long while to not have lived at least one grey day."

"You still think he is angry?"

"I do. Something has happened, that I know. But what can be so severe that even *Death* has lost faith in an entire world."

Azriel leaned in and left a kiss on her forehead, his lips were soft and cool against her skin. It felt like the first touch of rain on scorching summer earth. "Tell me how you have not."

"You assume I haven't?"

He raised a brow. "Not assumed. Deduced."

"Ever doubted that you're perhaps a bad judge of character?"

"No skill set required in judging you."

"Because I am an open book?" He'd told her that before, but she was wondering how much of what she showed to the world was enough to judge her character.

"Because you talk to the fiends and ghosts when the world has cast them out and fears them, you reassure them, offer them company, and even crack jokes they thoroughly hate while you expect nothing in return. You're sometimes grateful they are even there though they really don't have anywhere else to go. And before you say it, I've heard you tell them that. I can't begin to imagine how you treat the world outside of shadows."

She was about to turn the colour of the vegetable she'd been compared to all her life. Or was it a fruit? She'd forgotten. "How do you know they hate my jokes?"

"They roll their eyes at you. Some sigh, too."

She gaped, offended. "They do?"

"How do you do that, Winter?" he asked, pushing her red hair out of her face. "How do you remain so spirited in a world who has wanted to rob you out of it? How do you fight for others when no one has ever fought for you? How are you so understanding of others when no one has been understanding of you? "

"I have, I think. I've laughed for me, fought for me, thought of me. I think," she added, giving him a quivering smile. "You said that it is enough."

"It is. But I pity the world that holds you and doesn't see you."

⁘⟶

When they'd returned, Winter had quickly made the excuse of returning to her task, and then disappeared between the library shadows. Hiding. From herself, not him.

She sat between a hidden corridor of shelves by the far end of the second floor and placed the book on her knees, attempting to concentrate on the words and failing.

She wished she was afraid of the ominous whispers of curious fiends that had followed her to that corner, and plastered their attention on her. Shining a candle would probably shoo them away, but she didn't want Azriel to find her. Not yet. Not until she had cleared her turbulent thoughts that involved him, him and more of him.

A shadow suddenly fell over her and she looked up to find Azriel's dark eyes pinning her on the spot. "You're hiding from me."

"No." Maybe she was, after all. Winter realised she should have hid better, harder, further, when her pulse shifted as he stood before her, when electricity zapped down her spine as he enveloped her space, when every sense in her body was thrown off as their gazes clashed.

"And now you're lying to me. What is next?"

She was terrified. Of him. And the fact she was beginning to doubt her choices in remaining partial against what they were to face in only two days. It wasn't enough. Suddenly time was not enough. It hated her even. It hated her so much. She would begin to find Death's reasons severely unreasonable, she was beginning to resent him, damn him, curse him, and...and almost beg him to give them more time. "It would be better if—"

"Don't lie again."

"I wasn't." It *would* be better if they remained apart. For her.

He tilted his head to the side, a shadow covering half of his face and making him look even more terrifying. "Winter."

She gave up soon, lifting a hand to him. There was little time, and she didn't wish to spend it thinking. She'd done enough of it for the past twenty four years. Now...now she was wanting to live in that hurtful reality, though Winter hated pain, she really hated pain. "Can you come down here?"

Azriel took her hand and crouched down so they were face to face. "I want to bring you chamomile and biscuits and chocolates, but I don't know if they can fix this, whatever that is hurting you."

"It's alright, you brought me something else."

His voice was dark and hoarse when he asked, "And what is that?"

"You." Her ears rang after she said those words, so she filled the space with more of her truths, "I want you to kiss me, but we only have two more days to live."

She heard his sharp inhale, saw his chest rise like the thunder outside—as if it raged. "And I told you I'd save you," he said, and then crushed his lips to hers.

Suddenly everything in her body felt scorching, and he was the only thing that could douse the intense burn. She kissed him back, not realising she was only dousing herself with more fire. "When I came here, I took an oath that I want to break," she whispered. "But it would be a sin."

His eyes gleamed like two dark beacons, letting her know how to find him. "Then let's make it a good one, how about that?" he said, smiling as he pushed her hair away from her face and peppered her cheeks with kisses.

She reached for his jacket, undoing it and pushing it over his shoulders, marvelling at the hardness of his body under her palms. Her teeth dug in her lower lip as she looked up at him. "Maybe I should start praying to the Dark God."

He licked a slow trail over the column of her throat, and she could almost feel his tongue between her legs, over her spine, and just about everywhere. "Maybe you should," he said darkly, undoing her cloak that left her in the thin robe she wore under it.

"I would have taken this slow," he said, trailing his hand down the length of her and then back up, stopping at the curve of her breast and brushing his thumb over her taut nipple pressed against the cloth. He wrapped his lips over the fabric and bit it gently, eliciting a moan out of her. "Maybe I should take it slow. Kiss and bite and lick every inch of your body to see how it makes you sound."

Winter had been touched, but never...never like this. Never to make her feel as she did. She put her hand over his, cupping it over her breast. "No. Have me how you want me."

"And how do *you* want me?"

"Now."

Azriel pulled her on his lap, her legs straddling his hips, her chest against his hard one. "Then have me."

Winter took one moment to catch her breath, and then reached for his belt and then his trousers until she freed him of them. He hissed as she wrapped her fingers over his hard length and slowly stroked him, her fingers barely closing around his thick shaft. Lust gleamed out of his eyes as he watched her work his body, dressing them with specks of silver. She drowned in them, drowned entirely when he slowly reached under her robes, trailing his fingers gently over her thighs as if he could break her. But Winter felt like she was made of glass at that moment, perhaps he could break her. She'd let him.

Her eyes drew shut and a moan slipped out of her lips when he trailed his fingers over her core and down to her wet centre. In one quick tug, her underwear was torn off her body. "This is no damn sin. Look at you," he said, his fingers sliding over her slick centre. "You'd make any man, God or not, fall on his knees and pray for damnation." He kissed down her neck, marking

her pale skin with his mouth. "Nothing would be holier than to be ruined by you."

The words sent Winter over a very steep edge, barely letting her balance on it, barely letting her hold on from falling. She guided his length over her centre and began lowering herself, her breaths coming in fast as his cock stretched her. The feel of him was too blinding for her to acknowledge the slight sting of pain that came with it. "Az."

"All the way down, Winter." He groaned in her mouth. "That's it. That's it, Winter," he murmured over her skin, his hands digging in her hips, helping her slowly start to ride him.

She could feel him everywhere, on her skin, on her insides, soaked in his perfume, wrapped in his arms, and even inside her soul, lurking there. He'd always lurked there since the day they had met.

He guided her legs to wrap around his waist and stood with her in his arms. Bracing her against a shelf, he pulled her robes up till they bunched on her hips and drove inside her. He took her against the library shelves. Hard and fast. His hips mercilessly snapping against hers. She gasped in his mouth when his thrusts grew intense and he swallowed every sound, lavishing them around his tongue and drinking down her breaths until they were owned by him, until she breathed what he allowed.

She clawed at his back, breathlessly calling his name over and over like a chanting spell.

"You feel so good," he said between kisses. "So good, Winter."

A small sound made her eyes snap open. "Are we not alone?" she asked, burying her face on his neck, about to evaporate from embarrassment that every creature in the library could see and hear them.

"If you want us to have an audience, I can call them back," he said in her ear, groaning as he pounded inside her. "You want us watched, Winter?"

"No. Of course not," she panted, her nails digging in his back.

"Why not? I want the shadows and the light both to know of the crime I've committed by making you mine. That I've ruined the one thing pure left in this world. That only I can do it. That they are forbidden to ever want to ruin you. Look at me," he ordered, cupping her jaw and slowing his thrusts.

She looked at him. "More."

"More what?"

"Just more. More of everything."

"Do you know what you're asking, Winter?"

"Show me."

He did show her.

She wondered if the wooden shelves would hold; if she could hold. Electricity coiled at the pits of her stomach, taking hold of every little nerve on her body. Soon, she was lost in another abyss apart from the one in his eyes, she was lost in an abyss of mind emptying pleasure. She came with his name on her lips, her mind, her heart.

He held onto her body as if it was the only thing he could hold, letting out a low groan in her ear and coming inside of her.

They remained joined for a little while longer, his brow resting on hers as they both panted frantically.

Spent and nowhere near sated by the look Winter saw in his eyes, Azriel carried her to their work table and set her on it before pulling out of her.

Both were still breathing hard, unable to look away from

each other. She'd broken her oath as a priestess, and she was sure he'd broken something, too. Something that had that haunted depth return to his eyes.

She tried to look away when he took a handkerchief from his pocket and gently wiped between her legs, suddenly too aware of what they had done.

"Winter," a small voice called from the entrance of the library, and both of them froze.

Winter panicked. Suddenly struggling to gather her bearings, she quickly rightened her hair and her dress, and called out, "Clara?" Would she know what they had done? Would she notice?

Her small blonde head peeked from a corner. "There you are," she said cheerfully at start, and then waned by the last word when her gaze landed on the man behind Winter. The young priestess sat up straight, shoulders back and chin high as she nodded at him. "Sir."

Winter took one small step forward. "I-Is there a problem, Clara?"

She quickly shook her head and hands, clearly trying to dispel the alarm. "Miriam has ordered an overnight mass since we only, as you know, have but two days left. She asked me to come get you as well. I'm sorry."

Winter looked at Azriel who nodded at her, giving his approval to join the mass. She hoped he'd refuse and let her stay there with him. Especially after what they had done. She wanted more of him. More of anything he could give her. "I'll go then." Regretting her own shaking voice, she turned to Clara. "I'll follow right after I gather a few of my things."

Right after her friend left, she faced the man who looked like he wished he was anywhere but there with her. "Should I have hid better?"

He didn't look at her as he straightened the books on the table. "I would have found you, Winter. Wherever you hid. From me, you, the world."

"Then why are you abandoning me back there again after finding me?"

His eyes rose to hers, dark brows bunching into a frown. "You do not regret it?"

"Of course not."

"You looked away from me."

"I can't look at you forever," she said with an anxious laughter that wanned quickly. "I...I was just—" She swallowed. "Feeling a bit...uh, shy."

"What if I ask you to do that?" He said, slowly walking toward her. "What if I ask you to look at me forever? Only at me. No one else."

"We don't have forever. We only have two days," she whispered, choking on her last words.

"I will give you forever, I will make sure you get forever. Tell me."

She wanted to believe him, so she let herself pretend that she did. "Then I'd only ever look at you. Would you only ever look at me if I asked?"

"You don't have to. I don't think I've ever looked at anyone before." He put a finger under her chin and lifted it to him before kissing her.

Two days until the end

Azriel had sent Winter a letter through Clara, telling her to rest and take the day off after the overnight mass. She'd sent one back even though she felt bad for her young friend.

No, was all she had written in it.

He was waiting for her outside the library when she went that morning, dressed in a black coat, his thin black framed glasses resting high on his nose. The moment he took notice of her, his lips slightly parted, his eyes tracking on every inch of her, his fingers flexing on his side as if he was contemplating on grabbing hold of her. "We are heading to Fessas square today."

She stepped closer and grabbed him instead, holding onto his jacket as she looked up at him and asked, "We're going to the city?" She'd never spent more than an hour in Fessas, only had gone to see the city while she'd been waiting for the next train towards Uvralis Sanctum, but she'd loved it.

He brushed a kiss on her lips, catching her entirely by surprise. Him, too, it seemed, because he swallowed thickly, his chest raising fast. All of the sudden, the innocent gesture didn't seem so innocent anymore despite them having done worse the day before. "Grab a coat. I will wait for you outside," he said.

She sprinted to her room and rushed back to his side, making him chuckle when she panted out of breath. Winter threw her cloak's hood over her head and followed after him towards the train station that was merely feet away from the Sanctum. She could spot parts of it from her room. Sometimes she'd sit on the roof and watch the trains go by, but she had not stepped there since the day she'd arrived at the Sanctum four years ago. The station was barren. It always was except when Miriam left to pick up a new girl or to bring one back. No one from the village allowed themselves the comfort of the new technology to travel, and still relied on their animals as if to preserve that sense of time, which Winter understood—they didn't wish to be stripped from the comfort of it.

Their breaths misted as they waited in the half-broken station seats for the next train to arrive. The only sound between them was the creaking time sign that was being blown by the autumnal winds.

He took her hand and put it between his before bringing it to his lips and blowing warm air on them.

Chills erupted all over her body, she felt that to the tip of her hairs. And when he kissed all of her fingers, she couldn't help but squirm in her seat and smile to herself, hiding deeper inside her hood.

Tucking her hand under his coat jacket to keep it warm, he said, "You must be tired from the mass."

"I was tired waiting for it to end and come see you."

He let out a noncommittal sound as a response, which prompted Winter to throw a little glance at Azriel. His profile was harsh, as if cut by a knife, his stubble had grown a little and gave him a darker look. He was the most handsome creature she'd seen. "W-what is it?" she asked.

He was looking ahead at nothing, but his face broke into a smile and she quickly looked away. "Oh, nothing," he said, throwing back her words.

Before she would say something, the rails rattled, signalling the train's arrival, and they both stood, approaching the platform.

She followed him inside along the small brown seat corridor filled with a lingering scent of mints and cigarettes, still holding onto his hand. He stopped and pointed to a few empty seats. "Take the window."

"Are you sure?" she asked. "The view is amazing, you can even see the sea in a small fraction."

"I don't want to look out of the window, Winter, I have something better to look at."

She turned to the seat to hide her smile, but stopped when he tugged at her cloak and pulled her against his chest. Azriel wrapped his arms around her body and rested his head on her shoulder, kissing her neck. "Why are you hiding from me under that cloak?"

She spun in his arms and wrapped hers around his neck before going on her tiptoes and kissing him. The way he kissed her back almost turned inappropriate, so she pulled away and he let out a frustrated groan, trying to pull her back to his body.

"People will see, and I am still in my religious robes," she quietly said, blushing down almost to her toes.

He frowned. "I should have just kept you in that dark and dingy library and had my fun with you on every single surface of it."

She quickly looked around them, sighing when she only noticed an elderly woman loudly snoring a few seats away. Tugging on his hand, she pulled them both down to sit and then kissed him again in the small privacy their seat offered.

She felt his smile against her lips and stopped, cracking her eyes open and pulling back a little. "What?"

"I like that you want me just how I want you," he said, kissing her again breathless for long—so long that her lips had swollen and his had about a bunch of bite marks on them from Winter's attempt to break it off and stop him from ravaging her in the public.

They'd been forced apart after an older gentleman had sat on the seats across from them, reading a newspaper and randomly throwing curious glances at Winter and her robes, and then at their hands linked together on her lap. Winter had tried to pull apart from him, but he'd only held her tighter. "Az," she harshly whispered, throwing a corner of her cloak over their joined hands to cover them.

"What, my sun?" he sternly asked, not tearing his eyes off from the man who was now minding his business. Azriel, on the other hand, had not stopped one moment from glaring at him. Winter feared a rain cloud would appear above the man's head to suddenly drench him in cold rain and strike him dead with lightning.

Thankfully, their stop came next and Winter pushed Azriel to his feet before the train hadn't even come to a halt.

Even though the skies were entirely too grey to even blame the dreich autumn, the city was alive with colour and movement. Sophisticated shops lined the streets, painted in all shades of the rainbow and taller than any buildings she'd usually seen in the small villages around Urvalis Sanctum. People dressed in the latest trends and fashion paced rapidly towards their destination, a few others hovering in front of the store windows while some sat in the cafes and restaurants enjoying their meals with a family, or with a newspaper or a book before them.

"Where are we heading first?"

He brought out a piece of paper with some sort of hand drawn map on it. "Your little friend said you'd sell your soul for something called marshmallows. I can't allow that, so I thought I could buy some for you. She told me where the shop was," he said, linking their hands together and pulling her in the middle of the walking crowd.

"We came to Fessas for marshmallows?" Winter asked incredulously.

"If you'd sell your soul for them, I supposed they were important enough."

She blinked up at him. "You do know what they are, right?"

"Your little friend said they are small, white, soft and sweet, so I suppose it is some sort of animal. Perhaps a small cat?"

Winter threw her head back and laughed. "No, it is something you eat."

"If you think they taste good, I don't see why it should stop us."

"Az, they are sweets. No cats involved."

He frowned to himself. "I see."

"Do they keep you Mages in confinement?" she asked. "How does one not know what marshmallows are? One of the smallest but most pleasurable joys of life."

He didn't answer her, and when she looked up at his face, his features had flattened to that unusual placidity she hadn't seen on him since that first day they had met.

"Even if they had," he finally said, looking ahead at the city as if he was looking at people for the first time. "I don't think I was looking at the world, Winter. I thought trivial things were just trivial things, didn't know they mattered enough to make one happy or sad."

"Strange as it is, happiness comes in all shapes and forms. I'm sure you've just never noticed all the small things that make you happy."

"Happy," he repeated, his eyes following a few elderly gathered around a game of checkers on a low table under the dark shade of an ancient willow that stood like a sore thumb in the middle of the town square.

"Yes, happy."

Azriel was still looking ahead at the crowd when he said, "I don't think what makes me happy is small by any means. Short, yes. Not small."

"Short?"

"You."

Winter stopped walking, her heart beating out of her ears and almost up her throat.

He stopped walking, too.

"I'm not short," she blurted out, flustered, overwhelmed. "In fact, I'm pretty tall for a woman."

He raked a look over her body. "You are, but you're still shorter than me."

"I make you happy?"

For a second, he looked like he was contemplating the answer, but then he said, "I don't wish to say it."

"Why not?"

"The world might hear, they might want you for themselves if they know I am capable of being happy and that there is something out there that has made me capable."

She sucked in a sharp breath and looked away, feeling her eyes prickle with tears. Winter felt his arms wrap around her middle and his lips touch the shell of her ear. "So, I'll just whisper it then. You said happiness comes in many forms. Mine is shaped like you. Has a mind shaped like yours, and a voice I never want out of my head." He pressed a few kisses on her neck, his hand sliding from her waist and lower to her hip. "Among many other things."

Briefly, she'd forgotten they were still in the middle of a crowd, and jolted when she noticed a few people staring at them.

Azriel let out another low groan when she slipped out of his hold. "Maybe I should just turn you into a rooted plant," he muttered, following after her. "Then I'll turn myself into a vine to wrap around you."

Winter wanted to laugh, what he'd said was funny, but she often felt so deprived of touch that she'd give anything to be a rooted plant and for him to be a vine wrapped around her, even if he was poison ivy. She'd never thought about perfect death, the ideal death one might desire. She'd heard people wish they'd pass in their sleep or in a field staring at the sun. She'd just found hers. All of the sudden, she'd found her happy death. She'd want to die slowly, wrapped in poison. Held.

Winter took a few steps back to match Azriel's, and linked her arm around his, clinging closely onto him, her cheek pressed to his biceps. But Azriel was not poison ivy, he was jasmine and she was but a fern tree, flowerless. He was keeping her wanting to see springtime, to see him wrap flowers around her.

But there would be no spring.

The world would end with autumn.

"What about your robes?" he asked, yet he only pulled her closer and even planted a kiss on top of her head.

"Don't care."

He shed his jacket and threw it over her shoulders. Her frame sunk under it, but her clothes were out of sight. "You care a little."

"You'll be cold."

"I've never known to be cold, Winter." He planted about a dozen kisses on her face before pulling her north of the city. "Let's find you those marshmallows so I can figure out what price you've put on your soul."

"Will you buy it if you can afford it?"

"No. I'll make sure no one ever can."

That made Winter entirely too giddy. "How?"

He brought her hand to his lips. "I have my ways."

Winter let out a gasp when they stood in front of a store with light pink and blue coloured walls and massive glass windows framing a colourful shop lined with shelves and shelves made of sweets. She'd never been a massive indulger of sweets, but she adored their colours and she adored how happy it made others. Besides the dentist. Winter had always thought they never deserved happiness anyway.

She almost but all dragged Azriel inside. Abandoning him at an odd spot as she went to peruse the shelves one after the other, and returning where she'd left him with two paper bags of marshmallows. "For my soul."

He grabbed them from her and went to pay the cashier with the biggest and widest moustached grin she'd seen. The second the bags returned to Winter's hands, they were pulled open and a fat marshmallow was stuffed in Azriel's mouth just as he was about to speak.

She licked her fingers and beamed up at him, waiting for a reaction. "So?"

He swallowed as if he was swallowing medicine. "I'm deeply concerned."

Winter reached out on her toes and pressed her mouth to his, licking his lips and tasting the sweetness on his tongue. "Sweet." She pulled back and ate two marshmallows at once, barely breathing, but a sacrifice she was willing to make. She'd had one in the past four years when one of the merchant's children had kindly offered her one. Sweets as many other things that oddly gave people joy, all were forbidden for her after becoming a priestess. She sighed around a mouthful, realising just how many sins she'd committed these past few days.

Something tugged on Winter's coat and she turned to find a small boy standing beside her, his clothes dirty and torn, his feet barely covered by the scraps of shoes he had on. He put his small hands together and bowed his head to her. "I saw when you got off the train, you're a priestess. May I be blessed, miss?"

She lowered herself to him. "You may."

He handed her a small bronze coin. "I don't have any more to give you to leave a prayer for me at the tree of life, but would you accept this?"

Her throat felt thick as she forced herself to swallow tears back and say, "No need. You save that. I'll leave a few prayers for you. Where are your parents?"

"By the river. They don't allow the grown ups to beg inside the city. We snuck in."

And just like that, Fessas was stripped of all colour in Winter's eyes.

Azriel crouched down to the little boy's height and extended him the bag of sweets.

The little boy's eyes widened beyond belief as he took it from Azriel, and nodded a quick thank you before sprinting off to his friends waiting behind a small alleyway.

"You made his day."

Azriel frowned at the spot the boy had stood moments ago. "It was just sweets."

"Not to him."

"I should call him back and give him money. A jacket. We buy them all a jacket each and some shoes." He turned to Winter, his face panic stricken, nothing she'd seen before. "Did you see their shoes?"

"What's it worth?" the old woman behind a tobacco cart nearby said, puffing a few smokes in the air. "We'll perish in a couple of days, they won't need them."

Azriel's gaze hardened on her and then turned to search for the group of children, but they had vanished from sight. His voice was colder than the sudden wind that blew across Fessas square, "Perhaps the end is for the better. They will never be cold beyond death, never starved or afraid."

She put a hand on his arm. "Az."

When he only shook his head, Winter realised that something had faded a little from his eyes. Something like hope and trust. She knew that because she'd seen that look before, and like all the times before, she didn't know how to help him. Or if she could help him at all. She wanted to—more than anything.

⁕→

The moment rain had begun pattering on the city's cobblestone streets, people had hid as if it was rocks pouring on them instead. Except for one person. Azriel stood only a couple feet behind her, holding a large umbrella while Winter let the rain begin soaking her little by little, her hand reaching forward to catch the droplets. She stood there until the rain began to grow heavy.

"You're wet enough, little sun, come here now," Azriel called to her.

She was wearing a huge smile when she turned to him, the rain had soaked her hair, letting it mat to her forehead and cheeks. Small droplets of water clung to her lips, nose, to her lashes, some were rolling down her brow, cheeks and neck. "You're not wet enough."

He stepped right in front of her, wrapping an arm around her body and hugging her tightly. "There."

"But you're missing the rain."

He kissed the top of her head. "I missed one thing. And that is holding you." Azriel threw his coat back over her, and pulled her close.

Soon after they'd sat on the train ride back to Urvalis, she'd fallen asleep with her head on his shoulder and his hands still clutched on her lap. A staticky melody was playing over the speakers, the sound fighting with that of the rain colliding against the metal and glass of the wagon.

The man that had sat before them that morning suddenly faced them again, wide eyed as he stared between the two. He loudly cleared his throat and sent Azriel a discerning look. "She's a priestess, you can't pursue her. Have some respect."

"Make another sound that can wake her up and I'll send you to pay respects in a burning hell hole."

The man pursed his lips shut and pulled his newspaper open.

Winter squirmed in her sleep, a small whimper falling out of her parted lips, and Azriel had never wanted anything more than to be able to look in there—in her dreams and nightmares, both.

"Shhhh," he cooed, kissing her brow, and she let out a little exhale. "Maybe I should tell you," Azriel whispered against her skin, "that I might have found a way to stop *Death*. You can be the shepherd, my little sun."

She stirred again, this time to get closer to him. Azriel wrapped an arm around her shoulders and pressed his lips on her hair, smiling. No one had seeked his closeness before her. "You better be dreaming about me," he murmured.

"I was," she mumbled, yawning.

He stiffened. "You're awake."

Winter looked up at him, still resting her head on his shoulder as she reached a hand to his face and pulled him down for a kiss. "You're hard as a rock and very uncomfortable to lay on."

"I am," he said, tugging on her lip. "I could be more comfortable if you sat on my lap while I'm—"

She put a hand over his mouth, and slowly rolled her eyes to the man hiding behind the newspaper. When he made no move or sound, she threw her scathing look back at Azriel. "Later," she whispered, and then felt him smile against her palm.

They'd parted after arriving at the sanctum, he'd headed to the library after insisting she needed rest. But she'd been convinced to do so only after he'd promised that he'd join her later.

She shed his jacket that was still around her shoulders and brought it to her nose, inhaling his scent. After changing into her nightgown, she laid on the bed, hugging his jacket to her chest and sighing. Her hand brushed something cold, and she pulled it back to see his glasses still in the breast pocket. Surely, he needed those. And Winter needed to see him again even if it was for a couple seconds.

Not even bothering to throw on a robe, she rushed towards the library in her nightgown, hoping he was still there and had not disappeared to his room where others would see her roam and question why.

She halted just past the library's doorstep, hiding behind a shelf, frozen at what laid ahead. At least a dozen men led by Miriam faced Azriel. His back was to her, but she didn't need to see his face to know that he had a menacing look on him. She could tell by the way the men and Miriam shook a little and avoided his gaze, and she could tell by the way he stood, as if the world laid at his feet and way beneath him.

"I never expected your loyalty," Azriel said to the men, folding back his sleeves to reveal skin marked corner to corner with tattoos. "But I did not expect this either." A cruel laughter left him, and shock rippled through her at that odd unexpected sound. "I lied. I did expect this and much more. To contest me is one thing. To want to kill me is another. Do you think I've not studied every little trick of yours? You've been planning to kill me for decades, centuries. Only waiting for the right moment to do that. Was defacing one another not enough that you wish to go after my realm and my power, too? Did I not give you enough? Perhaps I gave you much more than you all deserved."

Winter's blood grew cold. She couldn't...she couldn't think what she was thinking. It couldn't be true. He was Azriel. A Mage. He was Azriel, *her* Azriel. He couldn't be anyone else.

"Is that what you have been doing all this time? Trying to figure out how we'd kill you?" It was Miriam who had asked. "You gave your word that you'd look for a reason to stop your plague!"

His plague. *Death's* plague. *His* plague. Azriel's.

"My word," he hummed, circling them. "What value does it have in this world?"

One of the Mages began choking, hands wrapping around his throat as his skin began crawling with black little insects.

Winter put a hand over her mouth to stop the scream when the Mage then dissolved into dust.

Azriel spread his arms wide, and a pair of massive black wings sprung from between his shoulder blades. "Kill me then."

Her skin pimpled when the air filled with magic. Runes spread all around where he stood, circling him, and trapping him inside. She'd never witnessed that type of magic—the type that seeked life, the same that had seeked her father's after he'd spent more than half of his life conjuring without care—the unforgiving kind. Thin thorny branches rose from the ground and shot towards him, wrapping around his arm. Winter pushed back a cry when his skin began covering and dripping with blood. In one click of his fingers, the branches disappeared, and so did the man who had conjured them.

Contempt filled the Mages only briefly because Azriel stepped out of the runes, tearing through the barrier of magic as if it was mist. "You all draw power from me, from your servitude to me, from your humility towards me, from the fear of my power, yet you think you can use it against me. You think. Yes, that is the problem. You all think. Never stop to question before doing so. Never actually think twice." He walked towards them, a trail of blood following after him. "Only because the punishment beyond will be sweeter, you might go. Even you, Miriam. You, I want to see beyond this world the most. Alone. Abandoned in your own sin. Sitting between hellish fire."

With one last frustrated raging look at him, they all fled towards the exit and Winter hid behind the shelves, not making out why she'd stayed and not followed after. What more there was to know? He'd lied. He'd plotted. What else was there to know?

She felt her eyes prickle with tears. He'd lied to her.

"Come in, Winter," he called to her from where he stood in the middle of the library, looking up at the glass ceiling that had framed the oddest waning red moon.

Azriel, no, *Death* stepped into the darkness hidden from the moonlight, the creatures of the library following right after him. He raised a hand in the air, and they vanished, leaving Winter alone with the dark God. This is why they had always obeyed him. Why the spook played only when he allowed and why the fiends never did anything more than follow her around.

He stood under the faint glow of candlelight, but she couldn't see his eyes. "How about I tell you one last tale, Winter."

She turned around and prepared to run. Only that she couldn't. The room around them was no longer the library, it was a vast space of black with no end and no beginning, illuminating only them two. He'd trapped her and she had nowhere to go.

"You will want to hear this," he said, stepping closer and stopping when she stepped away from him. "It will help you finish your task. Don't you want answers?"

Winter didn't say anything, refusing to look up at him entirely. Her voice was small and defeated when she said, "Yes."

"Seven days ago," he began, idly circling her. "Something that had never happened before occurred. A twelve-year-old boy showed at the gates of my land holding his four siblings by their hands. I'd not asked for their souls; they hadn't been sent sickness or despair either. Their lives were dedicated by the fates to be long and rich and bearing fruit that would contribute to healing your world. But their father had sent those five souls to me. He'd beaten them all their lives, marked them with bruises older than time itself. He'd starved them. He'd sold their bodies. They had not been able to bear the pain and they came to me. They asked for me, to meet me. They seeked my protection. Who seeks protection from *Death* himself? No one has ever before. No one has ever looked at me as if I were their salvation. No one has looked at me with pure adoration. No one is supposed to. But I gave them protection, and I went after their father's soul though I'd promised to never interfere with any course of life. But it wasn't enough. I breathed the air in this world, and it suddenly dawned on me that it had changed from when I'd first stepped foot in it. The scent was severe. When I walked the streets of your cities, I saw the filth that was tainting it. Humans. All of them. I saw murder and abuse, I saw women, men and children being raped and being made slaves and spare parts for the filthy to use. I saw—I saw what I couldn't unsee."

Tears emptied down Winter's cheeks, her chest hurting at his words, the shake of his voice rattled her entirely. The story broke her heart. The cruelty of it suddenly painted black over the grey of her world. The children's pain, his pain, she could feel them both. Winter hated pain. Especially seeing others in pain.

"All this time, these people had lived out of my mercy," he continued. "Mercy I'd not offered or desired to give them but had unintentionally done so by looking away from them. I'd had my eyes closed all this time. My brother, too." He stopped moving and stepped a little closer to her, and even closer when she didn't back away from him. "Why should a realm exist to waste away when I can simply claim it before every soul that steps my gates reeks of rot. How many can I send away before this realm becomes the land of the haunted, not of life. How long until I am forced to fill my hell until the brim."

She swallowed hard, the words still coming out choked when she asked, "Why seven days?"

There was one small moment of silence between them where he was looking at her like she'd spoken for the first time ever, and while she was trying her hardest to come to terms that that moment might be the last she'd see him. "I gave my word to my brother that I'd look for a reason why I should spare you all."

"And have you found it?"

His jaw ticked and he looked away from her, glaring at the darkness surrounding them as if it bore the fault of everything. "I found a reason to spare only one."

"Let me go," Winter whispered, her voice shaking.

And he did. The walls of darkness bursted into thin dust, vanishing in the air, and letting the glow of the library fill the space again.

Winter didn't look at him one last time as she wanted before she turned away and left. But her feet halted against her wishes and better judgement, and then turned towards the healers' quarters. Even her arms did not obey her, they picked bandages, alcohol, thread and a needle. When she returned back to the library, she found him sitting on a chair, hunched over, his hands cradling his head.

His attention whipped to her as she wordlessly approached him. He only watched her. Silently. Not moving at all. Not even blinking.

Not either of them said anything as Winter kneeled before the dark God and took his arm in her hands. He made no sounds of pain either as she cleaned off the blood and the wounds in his arm, or when she began stitching the cuts up.

"You came back," he said.

"You were bleeding."

"You came back."

Her throat thickened with a cry. "It would have gotten infected."

"I can heal my body in an instant."

She faltered, trying to move away from him but failing when she got pinned by his dark gaze. "Why didn't you say so?"

"Because I am trying to cheat the fates of every moment I can have with you."

It hurt her and Winter couldn't bear the pain. Winter hated pain. "You lied to me."

"Would you have stayed that first day if I had introduced myself by the name your kind has given me?"

"Yes." No. Yes. Maybe. She didn't know the exact answer. Maybe because it didn't matter. Not anymore. Not after all that had happened between them. Because at the end there was him. At the end there would always be him.

"But you would have been afraid. Like you are now."

"Does it matter?"

"I've told you time and time again, that everything matters when it comes to you."

The pain was spreading, and Winter was in agony. "This is not about me. It has never been about me. It's about the pain of many."

"There is no pain in death."

"Only cruelty."

He reached for her. "Winter."

She stepped away. "How can you serve justice when you punish everyone the same?"

His hand that had halted between them slowly closed as he retracted it back to his side. "Humanity will never learn, never care, will never want to better itself. It will be better if it all perishes before more innocents suffer." He swallowed hard, his onyx eyes suddenly turning a glaze of grey. "What about me? About what I feel? The pain that I carry. Does it matter to anyone?"

It mattered to her, but Winter would never say it out loud. She hated her tears, hated that she felt his pain even though he was about to commit the worst cruelty there was. She wanted to hate him. But how could she?

"What do your tears mean, Winter? I want to touch them and take them away, but if they are because of me, I will let you be."

It took every little bit of courage her weak body held to force herself and tell him, "They are because of you." She'd lied and she'd also told the truth. They were because of him, but he didn't have to know any more than that.

ONE DAY UNTIL THE END

THAT MORNING SHE'D GONE to pray, and he'd gone to watch her. Leaning against a pillar, Azriel hid in its shadow, and studied Winter. There was a strange look on her face. She looked resigned, tired; her eyes glued on the thick roots of wisteria while everyone else's was drawn shut in a prayer. She was not praying. "Look at me, Winter, just look at me once," he murmured to himself, desperate for only a small clue to her thoughts.

Just then, she closed her eyes and began murmuring a prayer. Her lips moved fast, and his soul sank to the pit of his stomach when he realised that she had nothing left but to ask his brother for help.

Azriel couldn't stand there any longer, just watching her.

Miriam was glued on a spot just outside the prayer room, in the middle of the long corridors lit by the oval widows framing the faint daylight that was rising past dawn. It was obvious she'd been waiting for him.

He walked past her, ignoring her glaring stare.

"You came for *her*."

Azriel's steps halted and something like venom filled his veins.

The High Priestess, against any better judgement, stepped before him, filling his line of vision entirely with pure human hatred. "What is *so* different about that girl?"

"Nothing," he said, truly. "There is nothing different about Winter." Not to her anyway. Not to the world, perhaps. He didn't care for her to be different to anyone. If they knew how special she was, they'd want a piece, too, they'd want to tarnish her for the fun of it. And if they knew how special she was to him, they'd use her against him.

"For some reason, I doubt that to be the truth."

He could laugh, but he felt too bitter to force himself to even do that. How could Winter testify for the goodness of human nature? The same who wouldn't blink an eye to have her become a sacrifice for their sin. "You find a sense of confidence in the fact that my brother will not abandon you in my hands."

"He will not allow such a thing to ever happen." She stepped closer to him, a menacing look burning in her eyes. "I invited you to his home to see how weak you are before him and before us and our faith."

It had always surprised him how quick they were to pit the two brothers against, how quick they were to assume bad blood between them. When the truth was, he adored his big brother, adored what he was and what he did, his sense of justice and his strong beliefs. Despite all that had happened in Azriel's life, despite the lack of love his selfish parents had deprived him of, his brother was the best thing they had given him. It was expected that the sons of Chaos and Order would never live a life of love, but he'd lived it because of him. And again because of his brother, because of his brother's pure heart, he'd found another love. The love that was about to tear him apart. "It was my brother who granted me seven days in this realm. It was my brother who let me decide on the punishment you'd receive."

"Lies."

"Only the end will tell whether I lie or not."

Miriam's eyes shifted behind Azriel, and he turned to look at Winter who'd stopped at the threshold of the prayer room exit, staring directly at him. He wanted to sigh with relief when he saw no fear there, but she was looking at him the same way she'd seen the rain that day in the library. As if she'd miss it. Azriel knew then she'd given up on him—on her promise, too.

Miriam dropped to the ground, sobbing, and grabbing his feet. "Forgive me! Forgive me. Please do not hurt me. Please!" she screamed and cried like a banshee, pushing that dagger that had edged between his ribs last night at the sight of Winter's tears deeper and deeper.

Winter's eyes filled with hurt, and she rushed to the High Priestess's side, helping her up. "Do not," she whispered harshly at him, half choking on her words. "Please."

"I did not hurt her, Winter. You know that."

She only shook her head, looking away from him and helping Miriam to her quarters. And he let her move away from him. He knew that losing her pure heart once would be losing it forever.

"You came to our prayer," the young girl who he'd often seen with Winter called to him, keeping a good distance between them. "I saw you, by the pillars," she said, shyly stepping closer. "I...I don't know if you know or not, but seventeen years ago, my mother, Genevieve Arthos, died giving birth to me. Have you seen her?"

"She was the spitting image of you, Clara." Azriel remembered every soul and every face they came with in his lands. Especially of the ones whose hands he'd held while he'd helped them step into one of his heavens.

The girl's eyes welled with tears, and she sniffled, trying to offer him a smile. "I will see her soon, won't I? In a day I will be with her again. You've said that all will be together in death."

"Yes."

"I've tried to be good, you know. I've tried to do good by my name. So I could be with her in death, too."

"I know."

"I am glad then," she said, wiping her face with the edge of her robes, and then her face filled with panic and horror. "Please do not tell the High Priestess of what I said, she would not take kindly to the words."

"Your secret is safe with me."

She turned to him just as she was about to leave. "I always thought she was right even if no one believed her."

"Who?"

"Winter. She always said you'd have a reason."

"And if it was not good enough?"

"Winter says no one's reasons have to be good to justify how they feel, but only how they decide to act based on them."

"She sees good where there is none."

"Maybe she just looks hard enough." A sweet chuckle left her, the sound just as young and vibrant as her. "It's not that she does anything else. She doesn't pray either. And she ought to get down to the bottom of anything by exhausting everyone with talk until they freely give their truths to her."

⁕ →

Her eyes were closed, but she was not asleep. She'd not been asleep last night either when Azriel had sat by the far corner of her room and watched her rest. But she'd let him stay there.

He knew it had not been out of fear because she'd eventually gone to sleep and even whispered his name in her dreams—in dreams that he didn't dare belong, but in which she still wanted him to be.

He could almost see his brother's grin when he sighed and dropped his head back, tortured by even the thought of her not being able to talk to him as she once had. Azriel was about to convince himself that Gabriel had planned for this to happen after recalling their conversation. Seven days. He'd promised seven days. He'd never asked why seven or why Gabriel had directed him to the Uvralis Sanctum. He wanted to imagine himself squeezing his brother's throat for an answer, but then his question lay in bed with her red hair all over her tear streaked face. And the more he thought about it, he didn't care to get an answer for that one—he already had it.

Azriel reached her side and kneeled beside her bed. She trembled a little, and he hated that the most. More than anything he'd ever seen and witnessed in the long life he'd lived as the God of Death. He put a hand over hers that was clutching the blanket tightly, and she jerked it back, holding it tightly over her chest.

"I do not wish to harm you, Winter."

Something that glistened slipped out of her eye and rolled down her cheek.

He caught her tears despite his promise last night, and her hand shot up to wrap around his wrist. "Please do not touch me."

Azriel paid no mind to those words, his attention had gone on her naked arm exposed from the blanket. At least a dozen thin scars marred the skin over her wrist. He couldn't think. Not one thought. He couldn't make sense of anything at all.

"You have seeked me?" he asked hoarsely against the heavy weight that had settled on top of his chest. "Why have you seeked me?"

He didn't understand.

Couldn't understand.

Winter tried to pull her hands back, but he wouldn't allow it. Her eyes remained tightly pressed together as more tears left them and more sobs ripped out of her.

He rested her forehead against hers. "Open your eyes, Winter."

"I can't."

"Winter, it is an order."

One which she obeyed.

"Answer me, Winter."

"It was a long time ago."

He kissed her eyes, her cheek, her nose, her lips. "Why have you seeked me, my sun?"

She sniffled and wiped her eyes with the hand he was not holding in his. "You once told me that what I want matters. But I've never known what I want. I still do not know what I want. I've never been wanted either. By anyone. My mother did not want me, but my father forced her to have a child. She then pretended I didn't exist, while my father pretended I was someone else entirely." Her voice shivered, "But that one time, many nights ago, I knew what I wanted. I wanted the pain to stop. I really don't like pain, Az. It was so strange to finally know that I could want something and that I could get it so simply. It was a long time ago," she repeated, more to herself than him. "I managed to get up and went to a healer, and then found ways to not get hurt—to avoid getting hurt entirely. I hid. I ran away. I hid again."

"I forbid you to want me," he said coldly, his whole body vibrating with another sort of anger. "I forbid you to come to me."

Her eyes finally met his and some of that odd ache he felt lessened. She did not say anything, but she reached for him, pulling onto his hand so he could lay with her. Azriel did not know what to do when she rounded her arms around his waist and buried her face on the crook of his neck. To desire, to need someone the way he desired and needed her, filled him with fear because he couldn't have her. Not after the decision he'd made.

"Clara told me that she spoke to you," Winter said. "She also told me that she'd heard you and Miriam talk. That is a very bad habit of hers, I've told her that, but I'm glad she heard you. She also told me that you didn't hurt her."

"You already believed me back then. You didn't need to hear it from Clara."

"I did." She held onto him tightly, her hands fisting his shirt and pulling him closer. "Are all the tales you told me true?"

"They are."

"I knew you were angry."

He pulled back a little to cup her face. "Aren't you afraid of me? Of what and who I am? Of what I am about to do?"

"I should be."

But she was not, so he did not think twice to pull her closer to his body or press his lips to hers. She was soft, nothing Azriel knew anything to be, especially a human being. And he was hungry for a taste of her softness, not to devour it, but to relish it.

He knew what desire was though he'd never experienced it before her. He just didn't know how costly it was.

Her small fingers began undoing his shirt. "I want you, Az. Anything you can offer."

"You can have it all," he told her, pulling his shirt off his body, and reaching for her nightgown. His hands lingered over the lacy front, and they slid down the curve of her breast pushing against the cotton fabric. They slipped lower and lower until they grazed the hem of her underwear. With his other hand wrapped around her, he tilted his head to claim her mouth while his fingers slipped over her slick core. "And you?" he asked, bringing his fingers to his mouth, and sucking her taste clean off his skin. "Will you offer me a taste of you?"

"Anything."

"What if I want everything?" he asked, hovering over her and kissing a path down to between her legs.

She gasped, her body arching to meet his touches. "I think you already have it."

He'd never had anything more divine in his hands. He'd never gazed at nothing more divine either. Nor from afar or up close. When he licked and sucked her sex in his mouth, and she moaned his name like the sweetest curse, he realised he'd also never heard anything more divine either. Or tasted anything more divine. He pushed a finger inside her and then a second one, pumping in and out of her, preparing her to take him next.

Her hands shot to his hair, grabbing, and tugging as she rode his face at the pace of the thrusts. She shattered on his fingers, soaking them and his mouth. Azriel licked her taste off his lips and climbed over her spent naked body, settling between her spread thighs and rubbing his length along her slick sex until she started mewling and clawing at his back. "Are you at my mercy?" he asked, trailing hand down the soft silhouette of her body and grabbing her thigh. "Or am I at yours?"

When he entered her slowly and buried his aching cock to the hilt, he realised nothing would ever come close to convincing him there had ever been anything divine before her. His hips rocked slowly, savouring every little moan that left her, every touch and mark she left on his body.

He pried her lower lip from between her teeth and sucked on it until a bruise bloomed there. "Let me hear you. I want to remember each and every little sound you make." He cupped her breast and pinched her nipple hard. "That one first." He sucked on it next and she moaned softly. "And that." Pinning both her hands over her head, he began pumping his hips harder and faster, and she threw her head back with a breathless scream. "And most definitely that." Reaching a hand between them, he pinched her core, making her hiss and moan even harder. He felt her grow wetter as he circled his finger over that tight bundle of nerves while he steadily picked up his thrusts.

"Az." She breathed hard and fast. "Please."

"I should be the one to beg," she said, taking her body harder until it began shaking, her mouth parting open as she came.

The sounds of their bodies meeting grew louder, the scent of sex heavy in the small room, but he did not stop, not until she'd ridden off all of her pleasure and he'd filled her up with his.

Azriel remained there on top of her for a while, his face buried in her hair, his body covering hers. He didn't want to move, didn't want to let her go. It seemed she didn't want that either as she hugged his shoulders tightly, her cheek pressed to his shoulder as she trailed her fingers down the nape of his neck and his spine.

"Aren't I heavy?"

She hummed and the vibration prickled Azriel's skin. "Like a bear in the summer."

He chuckled and rolled over on his back, taking her with him to lay on his chest. "Sleep, my sun," he said when her eyes struggled to keep open.

"I shouldn't." Her words slurred and her lids finally drew shut, giving way to sleep. Tears rolled down her cheeks and he kissed each of them away.

He reached into her small cabinet and pulled a sewing kit from it. When he found a piece of thick yarn, he took off a ring bearing the red stone of his land and threaded the yarn through it before tying it around her neck. "I might not be back to say goodbye," he whispered, kissing her lips. "I don't think I can." She stirred a little when he lifted his body from the bed and he hesitated, standing there and watching her. Not once did he look away as he walked backwards towards the door. "I'll see you from afar, but you're so stunning this close. This must be why they always warn to never fly so close to the sun." Azriel's back met the door, and he dropped his head back on it, struggling to find the power to turn and open it to leave.

THE DAY AT THE END

SHE WOKE IN HIS arms, safely tucked to his chest, and not yet at the end of the world. But something did not feel right. His body felt warm, his touch on her back felt mechanical, his scent was not his.

When she cracked her eyes open, another reality crashed hard against her. She was crawled up on her side in the middle of a salt circle surrounded by candles and colourful stones, hooded men and women chanting a sharp spell encircling her. That didn't worry her as much as not seeing him did. They could do to her whatever they wished, but not to him. They had wanted to kill him the other night. They wouldn't stop. She knew they wouldn't stop until they did so because he knew them better than anyone—he knew humankind was not capable.

Winter could recognise the runes surrounding her, they'd been painted and sometimes carved around her old house. A hiding spell. Anyone within the runes would be impossible to find. It meant they didn't want Winter found for some reason.

She pushed up, and spotted Miriam watching by the far corner of the odd room that looked like nothing in the Sanctum. "Where is he?" she asked her despite the weakness of her bones. "What have you done?"

"Oh, sweet girl," Miriam cooed in a stony voice, showing

her tenderness that had never come to her before. "I've known your purpose with us has always been far greater than anyone predicted."

Winter tried to stand up. "What are you talking about?"

Miriam pushed off the wall and reached close to her. "I'm talking about him. There will be no end today, only a new beginning. And it will start with you. Your life, for his. The other Mages are already trying to establish a connection to Asphodel, to seek him. He left a note for me last night that he'd leave our world and that he'd no longer claim its end." She sneered. " Lies. So many lies. Of course he'd rather watch it fall apart from his throne. Of course he'd want to catch us by surprise and feast in our fear. Until we can lure him out, you will remain where he cannot find you, where you cannot seek him or his aid." Miriam pointed to the necklace around her neck which Winter had not noticed. "He marked you. A God marked you. How important you must be to him, sweet Winter."

Her limbs failed and she collapsed to the ground again. He'd forgiven them? He'd left? "No, do not do this Miriam. You do not understand. It was because of this he threatened this world, because of this!"

"And humility, will it save us? Begging, will it save us?"

"This will definitely not. Don't do this to him. Don't hurt him anymore, please."

Her mouth pursed with disgust. "And let him hurt us? Has your soul always been this corrupted, Winter, or did you just give it to him?"

He'd been nothing but gentle with her soul. No one had ever been. No one had regarded it before. Winter had not realised she still had that part of hers until he'd brought it out of the shadows it had hid. "If being corrupt means condemning this, then yes, I am."

"Then this world will lose nothing important when you are gone."

Winter stepped back and sat back on the wet ground, clutching his ring in her palm. He'd left her with it. He'd left. He'd not stayed. "Then this world does not deserve his mercy."

They'd brought her far from the Sanctum, somewhere where the sun burned red and scorching. There was nothing for miles along no matter which direction she looked, only scarce dry trees and parched shrubs. She could recognise the red sand beneath their feet, she knew they stood where river Lethe started in the world of the living and continued through to the land of the dead. Somewhere in the middle of the dry bank stood the invisible gates to Asphodel that only the dead and *him* knew. They had brought her there to lure him out of his lands.

Everyone had gathered by the tall wooden pyre where Winter was tied on, hundreds of blood thirsty Mages, scared and curious villagers, all those from the Sanctum were there, too. The girls she'd called her friends stared at her hopelessly, tears streaking their faces as they murmured apologies and asked for forgiveness.

"It is alright," Winter mouthed back, trying her best to offer them a smile. It was. It was really alright. She would be with him. They wouldn't kill him, and she'd be with him beyond this life. They would be together.

She closed her eyes tightly and looked up at the skies. "Don't come. Don't come, Azriel. Please don't let him come," she prayed to the God of Life, too.

She repeated those words over and over even as they pushed the torch inside the hay at the bottom of the pyre. She didn't stop even when it caught fire and began burning the wood. Even when she could feel the heat below her feet or when sweat covered her body. She did not stop even when flames began burning around her body and licking over her skin. She did not like pain. Winter did not like pain, but she didn't stop and didn't cry.

Someone else did. Someone else screamed and cried. Then more joined, forcing her to open her eyes.

Between the tall flames surrounding her, she saw massive gusts of black smoke gathering near the crowd, and from them emerged him. Angry and terrifying.

The fire died in a snap.

Miriam vanished in a blink, turning into black dust that disappeared in the wind.

The Mages disappeared next.

Her chains vanished, too, and she fell to her knees.

With every step he took towards her, more screamed and more vanished, perishing from the land of humans and forever denied the one beyond death.

Massive black feathered wings extended from Azriel's back and he leaped in the air, standing above them all, his eyes only seeking hers in the crowd of thousands. More black smoke made of small insects spread from him, enveloping the earth around and the skies above. It killed everything it touched, trees, soil, and air.

"No!" Winter screamed, climbing down the pyre, and running towards him despite the burns in her body. "Please, they only want to live. Please, you do not know how it is to want to live and cannot. I know it, Az, please. I know it. Don't do it like this. Not like this. Not when they are so afraid."

"Do not ask that of me, my sun," his voice came, echoing around the land the sound of a thousand other voices. "Not when you have seen what they are capable of. Not when you were their sacrifice."

"It was my greatest honour," she said, smiling up at him, her dark God. "One thousand times over, I'll do it again, only so I could be with you even if it is only for seven days." There was something else she wanted to tell him, too, but time didn't want her to fall in love with anyone else. It had made sure of it, as they now had no more of it. Time hated her. Time had always hated her. How could anyone explain this, how time had only given her seven days with him.

His gaze softened and then filled with those haunted shadows again. She knew something was wrong, she could feel it and see it on him.

The earth and air cleared of the black mist, revealing pale skies and an even paler dry earth.

He lowered himself down to the ground and walked towards her, the crowd of people separating for him to go through.

"You stopped," she murmured when he halted before her.

He cupped her face. "You'd resent me."

"Never. I can never resent you."

"You would. I can bear my anger, but not your resentment." He rested his brow on hers and took a deep inhale. "This world shall have another chance at living, but something worse than me will follow up next after I leave. Whoever will be angry next at what humanity has become will be merciless. After I leave, there will be no questioning it, and there will be pain."

"Leave?" Her voice trembled. "No, no, you can't leave."

He kissed her brow, his lips lingering over her skin. "Do not seek me before I come for you."

Her knees weakened and she fell into his arms. "What?"

"My deal to remain in this realm expired today. My brother could only grant me this one moment to come to you."

She shook her head, not wanting to believe his words, her own ears, her mind had to be wanting her to go insane. "No." Her hands trembled as she cupped his tear streaked face. "No, no. I just found you. Ask for another deal. Seven more days. Please, just seven more days." She looked up at the skies and cried, broken sobs tearing out of her throat as she begged for his brother, "Please, let him stay, please."

"If I stay even a minute more, I will not want to go back."

"Then stay."

"It will ruin this realm. My presence will slowly kill this realm only you still see good in. My magic will plant deep roots in the soil and spread until everything is dead."

"No, I don't see any good in it anymore, please."

He gave her a lachrymose smile. "That is the one lie I desperately want to believe." Azriel kissed her and she kissed him back as if she was desperate for just one of his breaths. "Live, Winter. Live wanting. Live deciding. Live for you. And live...for me, too. Make it good, my little sun. Make it really good, I want to hear all about it. I will wait this time. I will wait for you. Do not come to me. Do not seek me. Not unless you wish to break my heart."

She couldn't stop shaking her head, trying really hard to come up with words and solutions to have him stay. "Take me with you."

"I'm not sure this world can survive not having you in it. For their sake, stay."

He disappeared into thin air, only remnants of his scent clinging behind, clinging onto her skin. "No! No! No!" she screamed until her throat scratched and blood filled her mouth.

She felt arms wrap around her. Clara and Alyssa hugged her tightly as she tried to grasp the air where he once stood.

Her cries never stopped.

Not once in the next few months she remained at the Sanctum.

Even years later, people could swear they heard their haunting sound echo with the wind. The ground where they'd once stood was filled with daisies that never wilted, never disappeared in any season or the harsh cold. The path over the dried Lethe river poured with more of the white flowers, and each spirit grossing to Asphodel saw a piece of the gift Winter had given to the world.

There were tales that followed after that day. Tales of Death and her.

No one could tell whether much had changed after what happened, after they'd survived the seven days. No one knew if they were even capable of a change. But Death had decided one was enough to save them all.

EPILOGUE

THE KETTLE HAD BEEN angrily steaming on the stove for the past ten minutes, but Winter couldn't tear her eyes from the view outside of her cottage window overlooking the small garden that she'd built for the village children to play in.

She'd lived. She'd lived through incredible stories and memories that could fill books she had once read. After all, she'd promised him. She'd promised him stories worth grazing the pages of a book. Winter had travelled the world, planted seeds of daisies and offered the world small pieces of her views. She'd become a teacher—she'd taught the new generations to see the world with colour though she still saw it filled with grey. Winter had been happy, as happy as people were after rain, still lingering and wishing for thunder after she saw the hot sun on the skies. But she'd lived for far too long and she missed him, all this time she'd lived without a piece of her. A piece of her had already died with him that day, a piece of her was already in the land of the dead. She only hoped he'd held onto it tightly and had not forgotten her like she had never forgotten him. Time had let go of the grudge it had held against her back then, but it had now forgotten of her entirely—trapping her inside it. Winter could have easily escaped time, but couldn't, she'd promised to wait for him, to not seek him.

Leona, one of Clara's little nieces, her neighbour for the past forty years, came inside the kitchen and held out to her a bunch of the white flowers she'd planted all around her home. She always kept the seeds in her pocket, spreading them here and there, and letting life take its course.

"For you, Grandma Winter," the little girl said.

"Thank you, sweet darling." She took them and offered the little girl a smile and a piece of candy which made her giggle and run away back to her playmates.

Even so long after, she couldn't help tearing up at their sight, couldn't help the small sobs she let out at their scent. With shaky hands, she arranged them on a shallow vase and set them on the small table next to her sofa.

She laid her head on the cushions, looking at the daisies and clutching the necklace holding his ring. She'd not daydreamed in years. She'd forbid herself from it, from wanting something this life couldn't grant her. But she allowed herself to daydream at that moment.

Winter only closed her eyes for a moment, wanting to let her mind take her down a memory containing him, but sleep took her away first.

Winter awoke with a stiff back and in the same position she'd gone to sleep on the sofa. But somehow, the cushions she laid on were stiffer, harder against her body, and they smelled of earth. Something tickled her nose and her eyes popped open to see a massive field of grass stretching for endless miles.

"Daisies," she said, holding in a tearful smile as she reached for one hidden by the thick stands of grass. Her fingers stopped midway, and she numbly stared at them. They were smooth and pale as they had been long ago, years ago. When she touched her face and then down her body, she realised all of her was like it had been years ago. Young. Her hair was red and long again, too.

She shot to her feet, feeling lighter than she'd felt in years. There was nothing in sight, but grey skies filled with reluctant rain and fields upon fields of green sprinkled with daisies. Winter ran, she sprinted ahead, searching, and searching. Her heart could feel it. She was not dreaming. She could feel him, too. She laughed and laughed as she spun on her toes, finally happy—happier than she'd ever been in the past forty years.

"Az?" she called, his name echoing like in a glen. "Azriel?"

Her vision blurred when he wouldn't answer her calls, it thickened by tears, and she couldn't see. Would she not see him in death? Had he lied to her?

A wind swept the fields, causing the grass and the flowers and her dress to fly with it. Her necklace floated in the air as if the gravity no longer existed, and the red ruby attached to the ring began glistening. Brightly, so brightly that Winter had to shut her eyes.

"Hello, Winter. I've waited for you."

She froze at the words, sucking in a sharp breath and opening her eyes. His voice—she'd always loved his voice and had never forgotten it even after so many years.

At the count of three, she spun round. Like time had frozen between that day and today, he stood there, tall, and dark and smiling like he only smiled for her. One step at a time, one breath at a time, she walked to him, her hands reaching to touch him as he was reaching to touch her. "So have I." She laughed and cried and laughed. "So have I."

He kissed her lips, her eyes, and her brow, and held her for a moment to just look at her. "What tales do you have for me, my sun?"

There was very little Winter did not like about *Death*. Waiting for him was one of them. And perhaps all of it.

The end.

ABOUT THE AUTHOR

Wendy Heiss is a indie author debuting with a new adult fantasy trilogy. Winter Gods & Serpents is the first book in The Auran Chronicles releasing autumn 2021. She has graduated with honours in Forensics Science in the United Kingdom, but literature has been one of her passions since she could manage to read and write. Despite being severely tempted to ride the Agatha Christie route to crime novels, she chose to follow the Tolkien path to fantasy. She forwent fingerprint powder for ball pen ink inevitably forgoing her parents hope for a good life and becoming what they always feared...a figuratively starving artist. Any whom and how, she likes cats, coffee, particularly that cr*p from instant sachets. Claims to despise mafia romance from the pits of her gall bladder but will probably end up writing one herself to try and outwrite the greatest line in history: Are you alright babygirl. Also, fried sweet potatoes, she can definitely eat some of those without claiming to be allergic to yet another vegetable. On that last note before straying too far from a simple bio, please read her book.

Acknowledgements

First and foremost, I want to thank these two very fictional characters I wrote about, if not for them, I would have not gotten out of that writing slump.

I'd like to acknowledge my author friend, Lauren, thank you for always being so supportive of me even when I do questionable things.

I'd like to thank some of my readers who have without rest expressed their love for my stories. You have no idea, but you have kept me sane in very difficult moments. I often read your comments and watch the content you make about my books over and over before I fall asleep. Jana, Oana, Ruby, Nadia, Yaiza, A.N, Aleksandra, Lexi, Cassandra, Ebony. And of course, Sara, you know who you are, your videos always make my day.

I'd like to thank Katerina for being insanely talented and for always taking on with my projects.I'd like to thank Margherita for being the absolute best and putting the cover together when I was stressing out about it nonstop.I'd like to thank my baby sister for always, always being there for me and for listening me rattle about these stories that I write twenty four hours of these blessed days.

Last but not least, Neta, Bonnie, Molly, love you!!

Also by Wendy Heiss

The Auran Chronicles
Winter Gods & Serpents
Spring Guardians & Songbirds
Season Warriors & Wolves
Autumn Queens & Shadows (coming soon)
Summer Heirs & Fire (coming winter 2023)
Daughters of Chaos
City of Alabaster (coming out october 2023)
Blue Fairytales
At the end there was you
The last war we fought (coming out soon)

Printed in the USA
CPSIA information can be obtained
at www.ICGtesting.com
LVHW020715260524
781439LV00044B/2068